ULTIMATUM

A PROPHETIC SCIENCE FICTION NOVEL

JOHN ANDERSEN

ULTIMATUM

by John Andersen

For permission requests, contact the publisher below:

Cayélle Publishing/Surge Imprint
Lancaster, California USA
www.CayellePublishing.com

Orders by U.S. trade bookstores and wholesalers, please contact Freadom Distribution:
Tel: (833) 229-3553 ext 813 or email: Freadom@Cayelle.com

Categories: 1. Science Fiction 2. Action 3. Adventure
Printed in the United States of America

Cover Art by Robin Ludwig Design, Inc.
Interior Design & Typesetting by Ampersand Book Interiors
ISBN: 978-1-952404-35-1 [paperback]
ISBN: 978-1-952404-34-4 [ebook]
Library of Congress Control Number 2020944881

First Edition

SURGE
Cayélle

OTHER BOOKS BY THE AUTHOR:

The Final Option [Bahamas]
Book 1 of the Final Option Series

Double Trouble
Book 2 of the Final Option Series

The Monaco Conspiracy
Book 3 of the Final Option Series

The Star of Light
Book 4 of the Final Option Series

DEDICATION

This book is dedicated to my wife, Suzanne, and also to several good friends, who for reasons of their own, wish to remain anonymous. Thank you for the help, expertise, and encouragement you gave me, and for keeping me on track throughout this project.

My wife, as usual, did a superb job in keeping the facts straight, and AB once again patiently corrected my many punctuation and grammatical errors to keep the story flowing during her proofreading of the drafts of this book. That being said, any mistakes the reader may find, I acknowledge are mine and mine alone.

Any comments, encouragement or criticisms can be left on the author's page on goodreads.com or the reviews page at

amazon.com. Reviews can also be left on my website,

WWW.FINALOPTIONSERIES.COM.

I check them on a regular basis.

PROLOGUE

"It was pitch black when they first came. The *stars and thin sliver of moon that should have been visible were hidden behind a thick, low-laying blanket of clouds. The wind was howling, and the snow threatening.*

"Nobody who was there that night could remember when the first confrontation started, but all agreed it was what started the downhill slide in which the Earth soon found itself.

"The appearance of a speck of light in the east soon grew to such an extent that it was impossible to miss or ignore. The people at the bar, situated by itself in an isolated valley, noticed it first, for it shone through the front windows and soon overwhelmed the interior lights, which were always too dim, anyway.

"It threw squares of light on the wall, and glinted off the mirrors and bottles behind the bar counter, causing the barman to screw up his eyes against the glare. Those on the stools in front of the bar noticed that their shadows were appearing on the wall behind the bartender. Thinking it was a jerk with his high beams on, they turned and looked behind them.

"The light grew more intense, to the point that they had to turn away and shut their eyes, for even the reflected light off the mirrors on the back wall was too painful to look at without squinting. Many noticed that the room temperature had risen, going from mildly uncomfortable to scorching in a short period. They unfastened their winter jackets and flannel shirts, and removed them, leaving the men, and one woman, wearing only T-shirts. They soon realized that was a mistake, for the exposed skin began to darken. And in the case of an old man, his crepe-like skin began to form blisters, which burst, giving the impression that his skin was boiling off his arms.

"Then everyone began to broil, as if in an oven. Water tossed on their skin evaporated immediately, and did little, if anything, to cool the skin. Most draped their winter coats over the exposed parts of their bodies, which gave some relief. But the temperature was still rising, and it became more and more difficult to breathe as they took in what felt like super-heated desert air from Death Valley.

"Two of the older men passed out from heat exhaustion, and the woman's complaint of feeling faint fell on deaf ears, for they were all trying to look after their own conditions, which were growing more desperate by the second. A couple of the men noticed the paint on the wall had started to bubble and smoke, and the wax in the candles decorating the few tables had already melted into puddles. There seemed no escape, for to try and run outside would have been a death sentence, as the walls of the standalone building at least provided protection.

"They all lay on the bar's filthy, beer-stained floor, and one by one, lost consciousness until only one wretched soul remained cognitive.

"Then it was over. The brilliant light blinked off without warning, leaving the room in darkness for the few seconds it took for their eyes to dilate again. The temperature started dropping, slowly at

first, then with increasing rapidity, until the people regaining consciousness were forced to start climbing back into their clothes to keep from getting frostbite. They were all in a miserable state, and the bartender, realizing they needed help, crawled over to the pay phone in the alcove. With great difficulty, he finally managed to get through to the local hospital to request ambulances be sent.

"When the police and medics arrived, they were astounded to find that the outside of the building was a charred mess and looked as if it had been through a forest fire, except for one unexplainable fact. The two-foot snowdrifts banked against the building were still intact and had not melted. Other than their own, the police did not find any tracks in the deep snow in the vicinity. They were about to dismiss the call as a hoax, when to the amazement of these first responders, the front door of the bar opened, and out trooped a collection of sun-burned patrons, some bearing first-degree burns to their faces and forearms. All twelve people who were in the bar that night were subsequently taken to the hospital, treated, and released with no apparent permanent ill-effects.

"Despite many theories brought forward by a new breed of ufologists, no one has ever been able to explain where the light came from that night at the bar."

The speaker leaned back in her wing chair, lit another foul-smelling cigarette, and took a sip of her straight-up Maker's Mark. She threw an enquiring look across the coffee table between them, at her companion, and raised an eyebrow at him.

"This event occurred in 1947, exactly one hundred years ago. The incident has been well-documented because of the unusual nature of the circumstances surrounding it, and of course, the official nature of the first responders. The bar involved is still in existence, and is located about twenty miles west of Denver, Colorado, up in the foothills of the Rocky Mountains. I have been to see it for myself, and it is still burned black on the outside, although it has weathered a lot. The people this happened to all lived a normal lifespan with, seemingly, no ill-effects, except for one who was killed in an car accident. To this day, nobody has been able to offer a reasonable explanation as to how the building got so burned on only the one side without the snow melting, and of course, what kind of light caused it to burn so badly."

Deep in thought, the man took another sip of his drink, then looked up, wearily.

"And you are telling me this story because you think that episode is somehow connected to what's happening now?" he said.

"I'd bet my life on it!" she replied.

He smiled at her conviction. "You already have. But now you're betting the future of the Earth on it, right?"

With a deep sigh, she said, "Yes, I guess so. But I have an even more enlightening story to tell you. This one occurred in 1997, exactly fifty years ago. One of the reasons that these stories are so hard to verify is that they all seem to have occurred in or around bars, and you can imagine the difficulty we had getting verifiable information out of the people who were present at this one."

Of the two people present, the speaker was the more powerful, being the president of the United States, Sylvia Han-Chin. The other, as well as being her good and longtime friend, was also the Secretary of State, Ben Williamson. What they were discussing at this impromptu get-together would affect everyone on earth.

After pausing to take gulp from her glass of bourbon, Sylvia continued with her story.

"It was April, after a long and harsh winter up in the northern states, and the people in Fort Lauderdale, Florida were glad to see that the snowbirds—large crowds of whom had been plaguing them all the winter—were finally going home, leaving the locals to the sleepy routine they maintained during the summer. It was just going on dusk, with the western sky brilliantly lit in shades of gold, red, and orange.

"Those standing outside the bar at the makeshift counter on the sidewalk, which had been fastened to the support posts for the overhanging roof, were the first to notice the arrival of the futuristic-looking black sports car, which pulled into the spot that had just been vacated by the van belonging to the band playing that night. It was silent as it maneuvered into the parallel parking spot with ease, a maneuver that most Florida drivers seemed to find difficult, judging by their haphazardly parked cars.

"The black sports car didn't show any manufacturer's identification, and a temporary paper registration was taped to the back window, which was blacked out like all the other windows, to the point of illegality.

"The car door opened, swinging upward instead of outward, and a tall, slim figure emerged from the cockpit. Despite that it was a hot, humid evening, he was overdressed and in all black. His cotton shirt, leather pants, and leather boots were topped by a leather duster and a full-face helmet. As he walked over to the pay meter to get his parking ticket, the door on the car slid silently shut, apparently on its own, because the stranger had not touched it.

"He walked with a measured and subtle grace from the meter, into the bar, and found a seat in the back, since all the seats in the front were taken by people waiting to hear Florida's premier blues band.

He removed his helmet as he took his seat, and placed it on the bar. He had smooth, Germanic-Scandinavian features, and was tanned, with startling blue eyes that seemed to glow in the dim lighting of the bar, and short-cropped black hair. In a quiet, rumbling voice, he placed his order with the bartender, and then turned to survey the patrons of the bar, who were openly staring at the stranger.

"'That ticket is supposed to be displayed in your car, unless you want a ticket,' said the man sitting next to him.

"'But then nobody could see it, with my blacked-out windows. Don't you worry, I've got it covered.' The stranger's voice, although low and gravelly, was surprisingly soft for such a big man.

"And his demeanor was a touch effeminate, as if he were a parent addressing a troublesome child.

"'So what kind of car is that?" the man said. "Who makes it?'

"'It's a homebuilt.' The stranger smiled.

"'You don't say? What kind of power?'

"'More power than any vehicle on earth.'

"The man beside him, seemingly satisfied with this cryptic answer, shrugged and went back to his beer.

"The stranger turned back toward where the band had finally finished setting up and were beginning their introductions. He smiled at the obviously perplexed patrons who seemed taken aback at this stranger's intrusion into their private domain.

"One large lumberjack of a man, clearly much more inebriated than his companions, for he had been imbibing longer than they had, stood and staggered toward the stranger, with latent anger on his face.

"'This bar is for locals only, so why don't you get in your fancy car and take off,' he said with true menace in his voice.

"From behind the stranger, the bartender said, 'C'mon now, Jack. This is a public place. He has just as much right to be here as you

do. Go on back to your seat and drink your beer. The band's about to start.'

"Jack yelled, 'I just don't like his face!' as he threw a roundhouse sucker punch at the stranger's face, which hit him in the nose.

"But it did not have the expected consequences. The stranger was still sitting there, smiling, while Jack was dancing around, nursing his broken hand, and shouting a string of obscenities at him. The whole place, including the band, had gone dead quiet as the stranger shook his head at Jack's antics, and then picked up his helmet, threw a twenty on the counter, rose and walked out of the place, catching the stares of each person he passed.

"'As I don't wish to disturb your evening with my presence, I'll be going now. But don't you worry. I will be back.'

When he got to the car, he donned his helmet, and as if that was a signal to the car, the driver's side door swung upward. The few patrons who were able to catch a fleeting glimpse into the cockpit all agreed later that that they had never before seen such an intricate combination of screens, lights, and controls on any car they'd ever seen.

As the door returned to its secured position, several things seemed to happen at once. Instead of backing and maneuvering out of its parking space, the vehicle silently rose about six feet into the air. The wide wheels disappeared into the body to be replaced by a solid panel. And the vehicle tilted upward at a forty-five-degree angle. With the sonic boom of displaced air, the vehicle went from a standing still to disappearing into the darkening night in a split second.

On its way out, it clipped and cut an overhead power cable, sending a half-block of Las Olas Boulevard into darkness, while leaving the patrons of the bar standing around with their jaws on the ground."

As the president finished her second tale, she once again took a gulp of her bourbon, and lit yet another of her foul-smelling cigarettes.

"Filthy habit. I will have to quit someday…when I get out of office."

The secretary of state was lost in his thoughts.

He finally said, "So who do you think that stranger was?"

"I believe the incident in Colorado was the first documented appearance of Charlie. Although, naturally, it was not recognized as that at the time. And I believe Charlie was the driver of that futuristic car in Fort Lauderdale."

"You cannot be serious." Her companion also took an gulp of his whisky.

"Unfortunately, I think I am. The second incident I quoted was easier to examine for the truth since there was physical evidence to document it in the power company's report, who said that the power line had been cut in between the poles by something unidentifiable, since the wires were fused at the ends. Such a situation, fusing of a livewire high in the air could not be explained away by any method available at the time, not even with a laser, and we could not even do that today."

"Has he really been around for a hundred years?"

"That is my belief. After a lot of extensive research by a great number of people, we have found that there are many more instances of strange occurrences all around the world, which would suggest that he has been playing his little games for quite a number of years, but with a number of imaginative variations. It looks, at least to me, like he has been here for at least that long. But probably much longer."

"God help us all!"

YEAR 1

PART 1

The farmer stood gazing in the middle of the barren landscape, looking around and shaking his head. What he saw before him brought tears to his eyes. Tears of bitter regret. He turned three hundred sixty degrees, and the desolation extended in all directions. Not a tree, not even a blade of grass, no life anywhere broke the horizon. Were it not for the narrow, two-lane paved road he was parked on, he could have been visiting the Old West hundreds of years ago.

He could not have imagined such baked dry devastation, not even a half-dozen years ago, and regretted his decision to come back to this particular place one last time. His fertile imagination led him to visualize that this was what the Sahara Desert must look like. But this was not the Sahara, because his farm had been in the middle of Kansas, near Salina.

At least, what once had been his farm, for this desolate landscape now belonged to the bank, who wanted it even less than he did. He should have known better than to take out that final equity loan on this property, which the bankers had pushed upon him. This property had been in his family for seven generations, but his primary motivation had been determination to save for the future that which his forefathers had left him. He had been fooled into believing that taking a gamble on an infusion of cash would allow him to keep this special place secure for future generations.

Where he was looking should have been rippling fields of grain ready to be harvested, if only the rains had come. If only. He realized that it was not his fault that the crops had failed once again, and placed the blame where it belonged. On the stupid, shortsighted, irresponsible, and ignorant politicians, corporations and multi-billionaires of the world, who were only interested in feathering their own nests and lining their own pockets. The scientists had been warning them for decades about global warming, and that this was what it would come to. But do you think they listened? No, of course they didn't.

His name was DuPont, Warren DuPont. But not one of *the* DuPonts. Otherwise, he could have provided his own cash infusion into the property, and would not have lost the land when the rains had failed to appear.

He stood still, listening to the breeze continuing its uninterrupted passage across the withered landscape. He believed that this year of 2047, was going to be one of the last years of viable survivability for planet Earth. The economy was on the verge of collapse due to the greed and corruption of the manipulators, which no government could regulate, despite their best efforts. Naturally, it was only those politicians that wanted to look out for their constituents who tried to reign in the excess, because many politicians were just as corrupt as the wealthy 1 percent of the population.

The people of Siberia were burning rubles by the millions in their fireplaces just to stay warm. Yen were being used for toilet paper, and the euro had been devalued so many times it took a person's weekly wage just to buy a decent meal. The British pound, reinstated after England's exit from the European Union, was being used to stuff mattresses in the mistaken belief that it was going to be worth something in the future.

It seemed that the U.S. dollar and the Chinese yuan were the only semi-viable currencies left in the world, and that was only because both countries were busy printing as much of it as they could. Every other currency in the world was worthless, to the point that printing offices didn't waste the time or paper to print it anymore.

Warren turned to look at the spot where his house, which had been built many generations ago, had stood before being destroyed in the three-hundred-mile-per-hour tornado they had experienced only a few years before. Only one of the many weather-related events that had ravaged the whole country. There was nothing left, not even the foundations.

The weather that had produced such a devastating funnel cloud had grown worse over the past decade, and this particular tornado had taken everything with it as it tore a one-hundred-mile-long path toward Chicago. It didn't get there, but was close enough to scare the living daylights out of the citizenry of America's former Second City. The Second City title now belonged to Atlanta, Georgia, which had outgrown its boundaries and swallowed up cities like Athens and Macon. The reason for its phenomenal growth was climate change and global warming, because a large percentage of people from the Northeast and the Midwest decided that enough was enough with nine months of winter, below-zero temperatures, and constant snow and ice storms. None of them wanted to go as far south as Florida, with its constant stream of hurricanes, so they hunkered down in the middle of Georgia.

Not that Warren had been there to see the devastating tornado, since by the time it hit the area, he had already been evicted by the bank, and had been living a pauper's existence in Denver, fortunate to be working in a grocery store. His beautiful wife and two precious children, believing his mental state had deteriorated to a point of no return because of his ill-advised loans from the bank, had packed up their most precious possessions and left in the middle of the night, and were now living the good life with a millionaire in Seattle.

Still shaking his head, Warren turned and wandered toward his rusty and beat-up Hover car, his sole possession since the bank had taken everything else of value, including many things that had no value to them, but had sentimental value to him. They did that out of spite because the farm and everything else he possessed fell way short of what he owed. His sense of fury at the bankers had long since passed, leaving feelings of loss and sadness.

He shook his head again as the disturbing memories came crowding into his head and threatened to overwhelm him.

Warren halted when he felt an unfamiliar tingling—a second sense caused by a disturbance in the air that he could not identify. He glanced around, but saw nothing, until he looked up. His gaze was drawn to a small dark disc falling toward the ground, its size increasing rapidly. His curiosity was aroused, for he had not seen anything like it before, and as he watched, it slowed its decent until it was hovering before him, drifting downward and left of where he was standing. As it got closer and closer, he realized it was not the small disc he had thought when he'd first observed it, but an enormous one. It was silent, smooth, and black, but with a pearlescent component to it, such as the effect car manufacturers get by adding silver chips to the paint. It also had an iridescent bluish sheen that accented the dark paint.

He staggered backwards. *It must be at least ten miles wide.*

As he watched, the huge disc started moving west down Interstate 70, toward Denver, still gradually losing altitude. He kept the disk in his vision, not a difficult thing to do, as he hurried back and jumped into his Hover car, which he managed to get started after the normal false starts and grumbling noises.

He followed the giant disc with ease, for it was drifting, allowing him to make several left and right turns to navigate the secondary roads back to the highway. He observed with quiet amusement, a crop duster with what must have been a panicked pilot, cut short its run across the field and turn a one-eighty to get out of the saucer's way.

Warren noticed the twin sonic booms, which caused him great alarm, as a pair of F-35s came diving out of the clouds, scrambled from the nearest Air Force base. After trying to establish radio contact with the strange craft, they unleashed a barrage of AIM-120 AMRAAM missiles at the intruder. They all hit their target and exploded, resulting in a huge display of fire and smoke, but had no effect, since the huge alien craft continued on its way. It did not waver, slow, or alter course, and it showed no damage.

With no apparent retaliation from the huge disc, the two jets became an escort for the visitor, because it eventually passed over Denver International Airport at an altitude of ten thousand feet, on its way into downtown Denver. It came to a stop and hovered above the Colorado State Capitol in downtown Denver, and hung there above the city.

Warren followed the craft until he was forced to stop by the thousands of vehicles whose occupants had parked to observe the phenomenon. Hordes of people streamed from their homes and businesses around town, because the craft was casting a shadow across most of the city. They were braving the early September heatwave, another phenomenon of global warming, to observe what was a once-in-a-lifetime sight.

Warren thought this would have been a frightening situation, but since the disc had shown no hostile intentions, it was more of a novelty than a cause for alarm.

Little did anyone know just how profoundly everyone's lives would be affected by this strange visitor during the next ten years. If anyone had tried to tell the population what was about to happen to them at this early stage, they would have been considered crazy, and laughed at by everyone.

At a thousand different points on the globe, this same scenario was being played out. And to everyone's disappointment, with the same results. The Russian, Chinese, Israeli, Saudi, German, French, English, and every other of the air force in the world all failed to make a dent in the oncoming ships headed for the one thousand largest cities in the world.

Unknown to Warren, as well the citizens of Denver, and for that matter, the rest of the world, at that moment, when all the alien ships had reached their assigned destinations, the annual meeting of the member states of the United Nations was being interrupted.

The speaker at the podium was being ushered away by a tall, thin man dressed in all black, who had materialized out of thin air directly behind him just seconds before. Everyone who had observed the sudden appearance of the dark figure jumped out of their seats and scurried toward the exits. Upon arrival, they found that the doors were locked, which caused a massive traffic jam. Many members of the assembly were in danger of being trampled.

The man in black took the original speaker's place and removed his helmet. He placed it on the lectern and faced the 193 representatives and their aides and secretaries. He spoke English, but his words were translated by surprisingly calm translators, into all the other languages used UN meetings.

"Ladies and gentlemen, if you would kindly retake your seats. I assure you that no harm will come to you, and all will be explained momentarily."

He stood with his hands clasping either side of the lectern, and waited as the panicked assembly members finally decided that there was no immediate danger, and returned to their places. The tall man glanced around until everyone was seated, and there was silence.

"While I do understand that my sudden appearance before you is certainly startling, I wish to assure you that you are in no danger, for I've come here today to help you, not to harm you." He leaned forward and made eye contact with as many people as he could. "My name in my own language is unpronounceable to you. So for simplicity's sake, you may call me Charlie. This name I have chosen from the language of your planet because I believe you should see me as someone friendly, simple, and commonplace."

He paused to let them contemplate his use of the word *your.*

"Just as you have been charged with representing the people of your respective countries on this planet you call Earth, I have been selected to be the representative here on Earth, of our Continuum of planets, which consists of over one hundred seventeen thousand sentient inhabited planets in this universe."

He paused as a gasp emerged from his captive audience.

"I have been sent here because of a growing concern amongst the people I represent that this planet has but a few years of sustainability left. So therefore, in an effort to help the people of your planet survive, I am here to help you and your planet come back from the brink of disaster, to a more stable and healthy state."

Again he paused to allow the assembly to contemplate the meaning of his words.

"To this end, as you will see shortly after this meeting is over, my ships have positioned themselves over the one thousand largest cities of this world. While these ships are substantial and impressive, they are not there to do you any harm. They are indeed the flying saucers mentioned in your old-fashioned science fiction novels, and by Earth standards are huge, being ten miles in diameter, with an edge height of one mile, and a center height of four miles. They are broadcasting this conference planet-wide, over all television stations, on all channels, and over all radio stations. We want the whole world to know exactly what is happening here today. These ships are also impervious to harm from any Earth-built weapons, as fighter jets from all nations are finding out right now. I feel compelled to inform you that there is one of them right over our heads at ten thousand feet, even as I speak."

He saw many people look up, as if they could see through the ceiling. He glanced at his watch, and now had a ghost of a smile on his lips.

"And speaking of weapons—as of three seconds ago, and by using the same technology that I did when I was transported to appear before you here today, all the Earth's offensive nuclear weapons, all the stockpiles of chemical weapons, and all biological weapons, from every country in the world, have been transported to one of my storage ships to be taken out into deep space and destroyed."

He paused to allow the implications of this statement to sink in, not only because he knew that some heads of state were slower at the comprehension of the current state of affairs than others, but he also knew that others would not believe him without verification.

"This has *not* been done so that you cannot defend yourselves, but simply so that you don't panic and destroy yourselves and your planet in a foolhardy attempt to get rid of us, militarily speaking."

He could see the looks of shock on many of the representatives' faces, and he felt sorrow and a little guilt at the uncertainty, confusion, and doubt that his words must be causing all of them to feel.

"Now, in conclusion, and in keeping with the objectives that created the UN in the first place, I wish to charge you with a most important mission, one that will go down in history, assuming that afterwards you still have a history left. If you understand what I am offering to the people of Earth, each of you will return home and report to the leaders of your respective countries, and respectfully request that they attend a meeting here in this chamber one week from today. A ten-year plan which has been drawn up by us for the salvation and reconstruction of the Earth, will be presented to them at that meeting. This unprecedented invitation is, of course, on a voluntary basis. But those leaders who choose not to attend the presentation will have no say in any future plans for the rehabilitation of your planet. A digital transcript of these proceedings will be made available to each of you so that no point is left out when you speak to all your leaders. Please stress the urgency of this request. It may be mankind's last hope for a viable planet. I will now take my leave, and you are all free to go."

He replaced his helmet, strode back to the spot where he had first appeared, and in the blink of an eye, disappeared.

The United States and Russia had much greater surveillance of the entire planet, including satellites, but it was the Israeli Air

Force that first reacted to what was perceived to be a deadly threat approaching Tel Aviv from the west, out of the Mediterranean. Although, the rest of the world's air forces weren't far behind.

The Super Mirage F-16 and F-35 Israeli fighter planes released every air-to-air missile they carried at the strange craft, which flew straight through the onslaught without any harm. The slow, steady flight of the huge ship continued unabated, without even an acknowledgement of the pesky gnats attacking it, until it finally arrived at its destination.

The Americans encountered several discs coming out of the Pacific, headed for Honolulu, San Diego, San Francisco, Portland, and Seattle. And several from the Atlantic, headed for Miami, Atlanta, Richmond, Washington, and New York. Some were also headed for Chicago, Dallas, and New Orleans. And Denver had its own ship.

Beijing and Shanghai had ships settling in. And Tokyo was also covered.

In Russia, Moscow and Stalingrad. And in Europe—Berlin, Paris, Rome, Zurich, Vienna, Madrid, Lisbon, Brussels, Amsterdam, Copenhagen, Oslo, Stockholm, Helsinki, and Monaco had a black ship hovering above them.

In the British Isles, the giant ship cast its shadow over London, Dublin, Glasgow, and Edinburg.

In Australia, Sydney and Melbourne were under the same umbrella. And Auckland, New Zealand had its own ship.

Cities across the globe were being converged upon by these massive, mysterious ships. The world's thousand largest cities now found themselves under the ten-mile umbrella of these ominous-looking black shapes. Despite what everyone was starting to feel and fear, no overt actions were initiated from the ships as they hovered above their respective destinations. Gradually, people returned to their jobs, their homes, and their lives, all while keeping a wary eye on the apparition in the sky.

As word of the huge disks spread to the outlying areas around the world—those without a view of the phenomenon, and who were relying on news reports for information—the mood of most people mellowed when they listened to Charlie as he explained the situation.

As with all political speeches, this one was taken warily, and with a grain of salt. Much of the world's population was skeptical, at best.

PART 2

As the assemblage rushed outside after the meeting broke up, they noticed it was gloomy, like an overcast winter day when a snowstorm was expected. After looking up, they couldn't help but spot the reason. The ten-mile-long alien ship was crowding the sky, with faint daylight just showing around the edges.

Surprisingly, few people were panicking since the phenomenon was displaying no hostility, and most of the people in the streets were just standing around and staring.

Urgent phone calls to their embassies had started the representatives' journeys back to their home countries before they had even left the UN Headquarters. All the delegates called for their cars at once, and created a several-hours long wait before they en route to their hotels and then the airport.

La Guardia Airport was unusable with the alien craft sitting at just ten thousand feet above them, and all air traffic had been rerouted to JFK. The majority of the delegates were able to make a connection that day, and by midnight, most of the rush was over.

But as they boarded their flights, none of them looked forward to confronting their leaders with such disturbing news.

After the last delegate had flown out, the alien saucers lifted until they were hovering at twenty thousand feet, allowing air traffic to fly unimpeded beneath, as well as above them. The first pilot to accomplish this maneuver was terrified. But since he landed safely, it was agreed that the airports affected could reopen, and that air traffic could return to normal.

Several hundred miles away, in an over one-century-old log cabin situated inside the boundaries of the National Forest in the foothills of the Blue Ridge Mountains, a pair of unfriendly eyes watched the broadcast, along with millions, perhaps even billions, of others. The owner of those eyes was Amos Richardson, named after his father, and he was a true mountain man, a hermit. He only ventured into Blairsville in Northwest Georgia once a month for supplies. Driving his old beat-up four-wheel-drive Dodge truck the fifty miles into town was an all-day excursion and an exercise in caution, for the cabin was so far into the forest that not even the tax man knew where it was. The paperwork regarding the place had disappeared long ago.

The five or six shopping carts full of supplies that Amos bought, one at a time, from several of the supermarkets and stores in the town, allowed him to spend a month or more away from people. Which, according to him, was much more than a blessing. It was sacrosanct. Not that anyone asked. No one had ever visited him in his cabin, and no one ever would. He always paid cash for everything, and since there was no record of his comings and goings, and nobody to question his motivation, he was always able to slip under the radar of officialdom.

Because of his age, he rose slowly from his chair after the programming had returned to its regular schedule. After the talking heads had their say, and after the speculation of what was happening and if it would ever end had ground to a halt, he descended the stairs into the hidden basement below his cabin. There, he retrieved from his hermetically sealed gun cabinet, his most prized possession, a Barrett M107 sniper rifle, which he laid on the table dedicated to his gun cleaning. He unwrapped the weapon from its sheath of specially obtained anti-corrosion cloth, and viewed his masterpiece for the first time in many years.

As he gathered the necessary tools to bring this shining example of the gun maker's art back to its pristine condition, he reflected on its turbulent history—through Iran and Afghanistan, and a brief stint in Columbia, before its final mission back home, the elimination of the despotic puppet of a foreign government, a wet work job in which he had played the leading role. That bumbling fool had occupied the White House for two long years, which, in Amos's humble opinion, had been far too long. Amos even had the heartfelt satisfaction of seeing the man's head explode from the .50 caliber bullet, through his sniper scope, during a three-foot putt, which the man had missed.

Let's see if you can cheat on that score, Amos had thought at the time, with a grim satisfaction that he had evened the score for the man's transgressions against the American people.

Amos no longer had a Social Security number, a passport, a driver's license, a bank account, credit cards, or any form of identification. His monthly cash, for the last thirty years, was delivered in a sealed bag to a box hidden deep in the woods, by a low-grade government employee from an unnamed government department.

And at the time of that money drop, the employee would pick up last month's empty bag.

The initial manhunt for the assassin who had murdered the president had died down long ago, and was the coldest of cold cases, for no trace had ever been found of the perpetrator. But Amos and one other knew who was responsible.

He had not yet had time to formulate any kind of a plan, but he knew a threat to the United States when he saw one, and he was ready to confront that threat, even though it would mean coming out of hiding and facing the new and different world it had become after such a long period.

The week passed quickly. Too quickly for some of those who were engaged in the security aspects of this unprecedented collection of world leaders. Never before in the history of mankind had all the leaders of the world gathered in one spot. Every one of them saw this unusual arrangement as a defining moment in history, and they were all determined to make the most of the opportunity to better their plight. It was left to the United States to safeguard the most powerful men in the world. There turned out to be, naturally, a large number of multi-billionaires who were left out of the equation, much to their disgust, simply because their opinions and comments were usually self-centered and irrelevant. Scientists, industrialists, bankers, doctors, and other specialists would be called upon as the need arose.

The morning of the seventh day dawned bright and clear, bringing hope of success to the thousands of onlookers who had gathered in front of the UN headquarters to catch a glimpse of at least one of the world leaders as he or she passed into the building. The world knew what was happening on this day because of the world-wide broadcast the aliens had arranged. Since one of the digital reports given to all the delegates had been leaked to CNN, they wasted no time in telling the world of the consequences of this meeting, and promising to televise the whole thing.

It was a logistical nightmare for the NYPD, who were responsible for protecting the visiting heads of state. That they were backed up by FBI, CIA, and NSA agents, as well as units of the National Guard was comforting. But as it turned out later, anyone with ill-intent toward the leaders had already been revealed and transported to holding cells on one of the aliens' ships. From the time each leader left his home country, until their arrival inside the general assembly hall, he or she had had a unknown cloak of total protection from any dangers, in the form of invisible alien protectors.

When the appointed time arrived, the meeting began quietly and without fanfare. The lighted lectern had been empty when they all arrived and assumed their chairs, with the delegates sitting to the right of their respective heads of state. To no one's surprise, the tall man in black was suddenly standing at the lectern, having materialized out of thin air. Like the first time, he once again removed his black helmet and placed it on the lectern before speaking. Everyone saw a tall, slim man with smooth, Germanic-Scandinavian features, who was tanned and had startlingly blue eyes which seemed to glow, and short-cropped black hair.

He waited until he had been noticed, and all the chatter had died down, before speaking.

"Good morning, ladies and gentlemen. I am glad to see that you all thought this meeting important enough to come here today. Even those nations that are not members of the United Nations sent their heads of state to join us in this attempt to save the world. Naturally, there are also representatives of many factions around the world, who are stateless but want a say in what happens to the planet. Before this meeting formally begins, I will give you some information you may find comforting. First, if you have been here before, you will see that the desks you are sitting at are different from normal. They have been modified by my people to include a small panel with a series of colored buttons on it. Part of it is voting, and part of it is queries. Green button is to answer yes, red button is no, and the yellow button is to be used by you if you wish to ask a question, want a clarification of one of my statements, or want to make a statement of your own. The results will show up on a board which will soon be shown to you. As reported by CNN, this session is being televised and recorded, and beamed to and from my one thousand ships in order to reach about ninety-nine percent of the world's population. All TV and radio channels will be programmed to carry the signal, and it will last as long as the session does.

"Second, I would like to give you a little history on my people. This will be for your information, with the hope that you will all feel more comfortable in the words you hear from me. Once again, the names are only my attempt at interpretation since the real names are unpronounceable in any of Earth's languages. We are called, in your language, The Brethren, and we come from a planet I'll call Ikentrar, in a system of seven planets, two of which are inhabited, revolving around a double star called Halesxe, which lies twenty-nine thousand light years from Earth, and is too faint to see, even with your best telescopes. This distance probably seems vast to you, but by employing what your movies call wormholes, and your scientists refer to as black holes, we are able to fly our ships across that distance in a little over one year. I call them *Time*

Passages. My people have a recorded history of over seven million Earth years, and we have been actively monitoring this planet for the last ten thousand years." He paused.

The president of the United States, Sylvia Han-Chin, pressed the yellow button and rose to her feet.

"Tell me, Charlie, if you have been truthful with us and have lived here for so long, why have you waited until now to contact us? And if so, given the abilities you've already demonstrated, why haven't you seen fit to help stop the genocides that have occurred around the world in the last ten thousand years?"

"Fair questions, Madam President. The only answer I can give you is that you weren't ready for us."

"Then am I to assume that you believe, even with all our troubles, we are ready for you now?"

"Yes, of course. Do you think we would have asked you all to assemble here today, which in itself is an unprecedented request, if we didn't think you were ready to at least listen to what we have to say, and hopefully, willing to take some definitive action if you agreed with our plan?"

"Thank you." She retook her seat.

"Let me continue, then, with our history. In the past, I have personally helped in saving a planet, which was in much worse shape than yours, to come from the brink of disaster to being a full member of the Continuum. Since I have done it once, I can do it again. All I need is the cooperation of the population of your planet." He paused.

"We are talking here about inaugurating a ten-year plan, starting right now. The first thing that has to happen is that all of the Earth's nations who have troops in foreign countries need to bring their troops home right now. Other than a small contingent to provide security to cover a country's embassy, all foreign troops must go back to their home country."

Russia's president, Boris Chevsonenko, didn't even bother pushing the button, and heaved his considerable bulk out of his seat.

"That is totally unacceptable!" he shouted. "This is something that has to be negotiated. We, meaning the Russian Federation, cannot leave the people we are sworn to protect to be slaughtered by their enemies. This is a ludicrous idea."

Sylvia Han-Chin stood up and nodded. "I have to agree. Without some kind of negotiated agreement, we can't leave those people we promised to protect without troops abroad. And there is no one else."

Charlie smiled. "Fortunately, Madam President, that is not true. When your troops move out, my people will move in. And they have a much better chance than your people do to bring about peace due to their superior skills and enhancements."

Boris laughed. "You must be joking. Nobody is better than a Russian soldier."

"Except an American soldier," Sylvia said.

Charlie gazed out with an amused look upon the two leaders.

"And ladies and gentlemen, that is why the world is in the sorry shape that it is. But just to be certain we are all on the same page, I trust you have both verified the absence from your arsenals of all your nuclear weapons—chemical and biological weapons of mass destruction. Your nuclear submarines are still running, and your silos are still filled with ICBMs. But the problem is, they have no warheads aboard. Am I correct?"

Boris and Sylvia glanced at one another and then nodded.

Charlie turned and shouted to everyone, "What about the rest of the nuclear club? Does anybody have any weapons of mass destruction left?"

He got several head shakes from leaders, many of whom had, until as recently as the previous week, had stockpiles of these weapons.

"I thought not. I have chosen to leave you the rocket delivery systems you still have, and you could launch tomorrow, but it would be like shooting blank bullets. The main reason that my people would be better able to protect those you fear would be in danger, is that my soldiers, like me, are indestructible and are can become invisible."

With a snap of his fingers, behind every leader in the room, there appeared a man in black. Tall, helmeted, and carrying a small box, each of the men resembled modern ninjas.

"These men and women are your Minders. They have been with you since you left your homes, invisible to all, protecting you from any harm that may come your way. Likewise, they will protect the people you leave behind when your troops pull back to your home countries. To me, this is the necessary first step which must be taken on the road to harmony in the world." He paused, awaiting any protests.

None came.

"So now we come to the first crucial vote. Will you, within one calendar month, pull your troops back to your own countries? Green is for yes, red is for no. Think carefully on this. Everyone, without exception, must vote, and it must be unanimous. A buzzer will sound when everyone has chosen."

A huge screen materialized behind Charlie, with the names of the various countries and three unlit bulbs beneath each country. A long time passed before the green lights started popping up around the room. A counter on the screen behind the podium showed the number of countries yet to vote. The green lights started quickly, slowed as the counter wound down, and soon it was down to two that were not lit.

Boris and Sylvia sat just a little ways apart, staring at one another, neither one wanting to be the one to go first. Even China and Japan had voted yes. Very few of the other voters had any troops overseas anyway, so the choice for them was academic. But both Russia and the US had troops everywhere, and it seemed to be a question of saving face rather than a decision of common sense and necessary logistics.

Charlie stood. He knew it was the right decision. And the leaders of America and Russia probably knew it was right, too, but their pride and the question of national security was holding quite a hand.

"Let me make this a little easier for you since you are both worried for the people you are trying to protect. As if the protection of my men was not enough, let me inform you that we also have the ability to establish a shield between antagonists that cannot be breached by any of the Earth's current weaponry. We also have the means to transport any individual, or even a large group, to holding cells aboard our prison ships, which have over one million sealed cubicles. Each of these cubicles is seven-feet-wide-by-ten-feet-long-by-seven-feet-high, sealed in one-inch-thick tritium alloy, which is the material our ships are built of, and which is indestructible. The incarcerated individual would be isolated, without a door or window, and the cell contains only a bunk with an incorporated mattress and blanket, a sink, and a toilet. A prisoner would be teleported into the cell. The food would be transported in, and any remnants out. The light would go on at six a.m., and turn out at six p.m. He or she would have no contact with anyone, would have no reading or writing materials, no TV or radio, and the cells are soundproofed. Total sensory deprivation. Depending on the severity of the crime, we would incarcerate him or her in there for a day, a week, a month, or years to contemplate the harm that person did to another."

Boris said, "How do we know this is not just a trick to make us lower our guard so you can take over our planet and make it your own?"

Finally, Charlie showed human-like emotion, and rumbled a laugh, which was full of mirth.

"If we wanted this planet, we would have wiped out the human race ten thousand years ago, when you were fewer and had no defenses. We have come here to give you a chance to save yourselves, not to conquer you or wipe you out." He paused.

"Let me tell you all a little about my race. Our technology has advanced to the point that when we are born, each of us has a tiny microchip implanted in our brain. This chip is so small your scanners cannot see it, and the technology behind it is what gives our ships and our bodies not only invulnerability, but also protects our bodies against any and all diseases, and slows the aging process. This gives my people a very long lifespan and a very healthy life."

"How long a lifespan?" Boris said.

Charlie smiled. "Well, I am just shy of one thousand Earth years old, and I am still considered a young man in my race. The chip does not influence our thinking, nor does it control us. In fact, we control it with our minds. Our evolution has taught us that cooperation is much better than competition, and concern for others is infinitely better than confrontation. Because of our beliefs, our abilities, and our way of life, my race has been chosen by a majority of the inhabited planets in the Continuum to be the guardians of the universe, and to come to the aid of distressed planets such as yours."

Sylvia hesitated, her finger hovering over the buttons. "I would hazard a guess that the reason you have given us so little time to decide, and allowed no consultation with our advisors, is because it will take a long time to change the environment. I have to say that I do not appreciate being forced into a corner like this."

"Actually, madam, I have never said anything about the length of time you should take to come to a decision, nor anything about your right to consult with your advisors. I guess that was an assumption on your part. But you are wrong on the second part of your statement. It is not the environment that will be hard to change. That part is the easiest. It is just about having the necessary technology. We have aboard one of our ships well over a million power cells, each of which has enough power to replace any one of your nuclear or fossil fuel power plants. And with a lifespan of over a hundred years, you will never need to utilize fossil fuel again. Since they only measure ten-by-ten-by-forty-feet, all you have to do is to switch the cables from your power plant to the power cell, and switch it on. It is self-contained and sealed, and no maintenance is necessary. These units will, of course, be given to you free of charge, and be replaced when necessary."

After a brief pause Charlie continued. "Now I know that, as in many cases, the hardest part of our plan will be changing the human mind. The human race has evolved to be flawed with corruption, greed, hatred, pettiness, immorality, envy, and lack of consideration for its fellow man. If it is at all possible to change the minds of the entire human race, I know it is going to take all of the ten years that I have been allowed by my superiors to accomplish that task. So you see, even I, like everybody, have others that I have to answer to. Not because of their power, but by choice."

What are the consequences of non-compliance? Sylvia said, "And what will happen if you clean up our environment, but fail to change the human mind?"

"Then when we are told that time is up, we will leave. But unfortunately, with your by-then advanced development, your marginal control of nuclear energy, the worldwide computer systems, your advances in space exploration, and your exploration into DNA and genome sequencing, we cannot leave you to bring your flawed mental processes out into the intergalactic community that we represent."

"What are you saying?" Sylvia replied.

"We would leave, but we would leave behind us a fire-ravaged, uninhabited planet without an atmosphere, and without life of any kind. It will be a burnt-out hulk of a planet. Just another rock in space. It is not what any of us desire, but something which the Continuum has promised its fellow members will be the only result that will satisfy them."

"If that is the case, I choose the green button."

With a sideways glance at Sylvia, and a crooked smile, Boris pushed his green button, too.

The buzzer sounded.

Sometimes things just don't work out right.

This was one of those times.

After Craig Simmons's honorable discharge from the Marine Corps, after serving in Sri Lanka and Indonesia, he had returned to civilian life unprepared for the downturn in the economy, in which his desperate attempts to secure gainful employment had failed. Although he had been able to save some money from his seven years in uniform, it was not going to last long.

As he went to places advertising employment, he could not help but notice all the veterans who lived on the streets, begging for their daily bread. He was determined not to join their ranks. Although, he had no idea how he was going to accomplish that. At least for now, he was able to sleep in a bed each night, even though it was in cheap hotels, and was able to keep up a neat appearance.

As winter approached, he found himself working his way down the eastern seaboard, along with countless others, toward Florida. He had never been to Florida before, and had no idea about the job prospects in that state. Craig just knew that if he was forced out onto the streets, he would rather be living in a hot climate since his service in the desert had robbed him of his ability to withstand the cold.

Arriving in downtown Ft. Lauderdale on a Sunday afternoon, he stepped off the Greyhound bus that, hopefully, had brought him to a new life. But he was already discouraged by the hordes of homeless people camping in the park next to the city library. Standing alone in the late afternoon sunshine, he gazed around at his new surroundings, disoriented.

Craig had chosen Ft. Lauderdale because Palm Beach had seemed too rich and pretentious, and Miami had seemed too dangerous. Besides, he didn't speak Spanish, and he didn't have much money left to live on.

After securing accommodation for the night at a rundown motel across from a strip mall in a seedy section of the city, he wandered over the Intracoastal Waterway Bridge at Las Olas Boulevard, off U.S. 1, down to the beach. Tomorrow was early enough to start the job search. He found a small but clean restaurant, not crowded at this hour, and decided on an early dinner. After taking an outside seat, he watched as beach life swirled around him, and took note of the contrasts in the people who occupied this stretch of sand, from the teenage girls sporting the brief bikinis, to the old retirees in their Bermuda shorts and colorful Hawaiian shirts, and everyone in between.

A noisy confrontation grabbed his attention, seemingly coming from the rear of the establishment, but erupted into the open air beside his seat. Craig jumped to his feet when a body came hurtling out of the alley and crashed into his table, followed by an enormous, enraged black man.

"If I told you once, I told you a thousand times! Don't come 'round here no more!" he yelled at the helpless figure lying under the table, quivering.

The little white guy in the tattered T-shirt and stained shorts cringed back, trying to burrow further under the overturned table as the black man reached down, grabbed his ankle, and pulled him along.

"Get yo sorry ass and them drugs out of my place, now!" He dragged the whimpering man out onto the sidewalk, flipped him over onto his back, and towered over the disheveled man.

The few patrons all watched this display without so much as a murmur. It seemed to be the normal course of events, or maybe the evening's entertainment.

Time stood still until the skinny white guy rolled over and crawled away. Craig could see the desire to kick him once more in the black man's eyes, but he restrained himself. He just stood and watched, and finally calmed down as the man regained his feet and hurried away.

"Sorry 'bout that, folks. Show's over." The black man righted the overturned table and then the chair, which he held out for Craig, who sat. "Dinner is on the house, for your troubles."

He then turned, and after speaking to a few of the patrons, walked back into the kitchen.

Craig shifted in the seat, glancing around at some of the other patrons, who seemed to be a mixed group. Some old. Or older, at least. And a few young people, with a fifty-fifty mix of male and female. With a quick assessment of the clientele, he was surprised by a short, wiry, bearded and bespectacled man at the next table, who addressed his gaze.

"Don't worry about that little confrontation. Happens with regularity around here. Name's Phil, and that man mountain is Robbie. He owns this place, and is also the cook. If I heard right, dinner is on him. And while it ain't on the menu, he does a great T-bone steak to perfection."

"Hi, my name is Craig, and I'm new in town. Thanks for the advice, I think that would hit the spot."

A shapely young waitress hustled up to his table, smiling, and producing an order book.

"What can I get for you, sir?"

Craig hesitated. "A beer and a T-bone steak. Medium, with all the fixings, please."

She rounded on the man sitting at the next table. "You've been shooting your mouth off again, haven't you, Phil? You know Robbie keeps those steaks for special customers."

"The least I can do for an ex-Marine. And Robbie said the dinner is on the house." Phil sat back in his chair, a wide grin on his face.

She looked at each man through narrow eyes, then shrugged and wrote down the order.

"And what kind of beer would you like, sir?"

"Don't want any of that watered-down beer the big breweries put out," Craig replied. "Please bring me an IPA."

"We have Goose Island."

"That works for me."

"OK. I'll be right back." She turned, and with a bounce in her step, went to fulfill his order.

Craig turned towards the other table. "So Phil, how in the hell did you know I was ex-Marine Corps?"

"It takes one to know one. I was in the third Gulf War against Iran. Stayed lucky and got out in 2023, and I'm still kicking. You got that look, you know. Been out long?"

"Six months."

They were interrupted by the waitress bringing two beers to them. She apparently knew what Phil preferred.

"There you go, gents." She turned to Craig. "I'm Katarina, and I'll be your server tonight. And hopefully for a long time to come."

"Craig." He held out his hand, which she took in a soft but vise-like grip.

A short while later, Robbie appeared, bearing a huge platter upon which sat an oversized T-bone steak, a baked potato, a salad, and a mound of mixed vegetables.

"All right. Who's the asshole that ordered this?"

"That would be me, sir," Craig said.

He did not want a confrontation, especially with someone who could probably beat him to a pulp, despite his training.

Robbie glared at him, and then grinned, the light of his smile spreading across his face like a sunrise.

"You've been talking to Phil, haven't you?"

"And a wonderful conversation it has been." Craig also grinned from ear to ear.

"Eat your dinner, and when you're done, come in back and see me. I might have a proposition for you."

As Phil had said, the steak was done to perfection, and Craig took his time, savoring every mouthful.

He finished every last piece, and when he was sated, he ordered and emptied another IPA and sat back feeling better than he had in months. Even the price was right. During his recovery from the enormous meal, Phil disappeared for a few minutes, supposedly for a bathroom break, but soon returned.

Craig sat back, admiring the happy circumstances before him. Eventually, his sense of propriety and duty compelled him to rise from his chair and stroll toward the kitchen, watched intently by Katarina, who had an agenda of her own.

He inched into what was probably Robbie's primary domain, and waited to be noticed. The kitchen was busy, but eventually things slowed to the point where the other cooks took over, and Robbie, with a slight shift of his head, invited Craig into his inner sanctum in the back room.

Robbie planted his bulk into an oversized chair probably built especially for him, and rolled the combination behind a huge desk which took up half the room.

"People have been telling me for quite some time now that I need to hire some protection around here, seeing what has been happening around the world. I still feel I can take care of it by myself. But a lot of my customers, Phil among them, feel that more protection would make everyone feel a whole lot better. To that end, I would like, on Phil's recommendation, to offer you a job here as a protection specialist, to take care of security for this establishment." Robbie smiled at Craig's obvious confusion. "I am a Harvard University graduate, an MIT economics major, and a successful commodities trader. Don't ever judge a book by its cover. What I can only offer you is this—minimum wage, plus a share of the tips, and a small apartment above this restaurant, free of charge. It's only a bedroom, bath, and kitchen in an efficiency apartment, but it is right here. I hope you take it, but I can understand if you pass."

"I'll take your offer. When do I start?"

"Right now."

"Okay, but first I'll have to go and collect my kit from my hotel."

"Sure, go ahead. When you come back, get settled, and then you can work a short shift tonight, OK?"

"OK."

Craig left the kitchen and moved back to his table, next to Phil. On the way, he caught Katarina gazing wistfully at him.

"Well, are you taking the job or what?" Phil said.

"What job?"

"Oh, come on. The security job I lined up for you."

Craig grinned. "Yes, I took it. And thank you."

"Oh, great! Katarina will be so pleased to hear that."

"What? Why would Katarina care? What have you two been hatching here?"

"Well, Katarina asked me to ask Robbie to offer you the job. Since there is nothing around here that doesn't come to pass if Katarina asks for it to happen, it was a foregone conclusion that you would get the job. Or at least get the job offer."

"Katarina?"

Phil nodded. "Katarina is Robbie's daughter."

"But she's white."

"White mother, black father. Happens often around here. She's really the one in charge. Even Robbie will admit that."

Craig shook his head. "What have I walked into here?"

"You don't have to stay, you know. I just know that Katarina would be mighty disappointed if you left now." Phil seemed disappointed, too.

"OK, I'll get my stuff from my hotel and be right back. I'm working tonight. But you probably know that already."

Phil grinned and waved him away.

Right before Craig exited the restaurant, he was confronted by Katarina.

"You are going to take the job, aren't you?" she said, with hope in her eyes.

He looked at her. "Yes. I'm just going to get my things. I'll be back shortly."

"Good. I'll see you."

It took thirty minutes for him to collect his kit and return, but in that short time, the atmosphere had changed dramatically. Slouched at the bar were three rough-looking males scowling at the other diners seated at the tables surrounding the three undesirable patrons.

Trouble was brewing.

Oh, well. I guess this is what I'm being paid for.

Craig used the key Robbie had given him earlier in the day, deposited his kit in the efficiency above, and returned. The situation hadn't gotten any better, but he made no overt moves, watching from a short distance away.

The middle man of the trio pushed back his barstool and stood. He turned and surveyed the room, and spotted Katarina taking an order. He sneered and started toward her. She turned and saw him coming, and tried to move in the opposite direction, using tables and customers to block his advance, without much success.

"Hey, mulatto, you gonna take my order."

She stopped and turned to glare at him, and gave him the universal one-finger salute.

The man advanced toward her, scowling, with murder in his eyes and his hands outstretched toward her throat. She backpedaled toward the kitchen, and he would have caught her, but Craig grabbed his arm and swung him around to deliver a haymaker which broke his nose and sent him sprawling backward. He hit the back of his head on the bar on his way to the floor, and arrived there out cold.

Craig found himself gripped from behind in a bear hug by the second of the trio, and swung around in the opposite direction. He spotted the third of the trio lining him up for a punch to the face, but before it could be delivered, Craig struck his combat boot into the man's gonads. The man dropped to the floor and lay whimpering and writhing as Craig turned his attention to the bear hugger.

A gong sounded, and Craig felt the bear hug slacken and then release. He swung around and found a grinning Robbie standing there holding a misshapen and battered frying pan.

"And that is how it is done." He dialed 911.

Craig crossed over to Katarina. "Are you all right?" He place his hands on her shoulders.

"Yes, I'm OK. Just shaken. I didn't think. I just reacted to his slur."

"I understand."

"Do you?"

"Phil told me about you and Robbie." He noticed a subtle change in her eyes.

"And you are OK with it?"

"Yes, of course." He placed his hands on her shoulders and gave her an encouraging squeeze while gazing into her eyes.

Somewhere in the back of his reptilian brain, a feeling emerged that had lain dormant for far too long.

Eventually, the police arrived, took the statements from the witnesses, and hauled the trio to the hospital, and then to jail. The rest of the night was quiet.

Craig and Phil sat together at the bar as Robbie closed the place for the night. He joined them later and handed them each a beer.

"Does this happen often around here?" Craig said.

"Not regularly. But sometimes," Robbie replied. "You did a good job tonight. Thank you for saving my daughter."

"You're welcome. Just doing my job."

Katarina joined them after locking the receipts away in the safe.

"So Craig, what is your take on this alien thing that's going on at the UN?" she said.

"I don't have a clue. I only saw the original broadcast, which didn't reveal much. I was traveling and didn't catch the meeting that was held a week later."

"I have it on DVR, if you are not too tired," Robbie said. "I'd like to get your take on it."

"OK."

Robbie ran the footage on one of the big flat screens, and then led the discussion of the implications of the aliens' intentions for being here on Earth.

Craig said, "I think I am extremely lucky to have left the service when I did and find this position before the glut of servicemen that is sure to come finally hits the streets. With everyone in the armed forces coming home, there will surely be mass discharges, and they will all be looking for employment. While I wish them the best, I'm glad to be here."

Robbie nodded. "I know you have only been here for one day, but already I am impressed with your thinking and your ability to handle things. I thank you for the way you stepped up and took care of the situation tonight."

"You are more than welcome. And I can tell you, I'm already feel comfortable here. I hope I'm able stay for a long time."

The grin on Katarina's face told her feelings. As a result, she had to turn away in embarrassment.

Craig's surprised delight was tempered by her being the boss's daughter. Still, he was mystified by her reaction.

After a spirited discussion between them that lasted into the wee hours of the morning, Craig decided it was time to retire. He walked the stairs to his small efficiency above the restaurant, thanking his lucky stars that he had been fortunate enough to find such an excellent position on his first day in this city. Upon looking into the closet, he was surprised to find sheets and pillows, and made up the queen-sized bed, which took up a good portion of the room. He stripped and showered before slipping naked between the sheets, and was just dozing off when a soft knock sounded on his door.

He rose and knotted a towel around his waist as he approached the door.

"Who is it?"

"Katarina."

He opened the door, and saw her standing in the hallway, still dressed in her work clothes, and wearing a shy smile. Her head was lowered, but her intention was clear. Craig stood aside, and she entered.

"I was just locking up, and I wanted to make sure you had *everything* you needed."

"Robbie?"

"He's gone home, as usual. He usually leaves me to lock up, which I normally do from the outside. But tonight I wanted to do it from the inside."

"Why?"

"If you have to ask, you have missed all the signals I've been sending you all night. From the moment I laid eyes on you, I've been telling myself, I have got to get a piece of that. So here I am. And if you have any of those macho ideas that a woman cannot be the aggressor, you better get rid of them right now, mister."

Mouth open, flabbergasted, he watched as she slipped out of her shorts and T-shirt, dropping them on the floor, and unhooked her bra, leaving her standing there in a pair of lace panties. Noting that he had the appropriate male reaction to her nakedness, she walked over to him and released his towel, which fell to the floor.

He kneeled before her to bring her panties down to her ankles before picking her up and carrying her to the bed. He lay beside her, stroking her breasts with one hand, and lifting her head with the other to bring their lips together. Both of their bodies responded to that lingering kiss, and soon nature took them on a ride that neither would soon forget.

They were both exhausted when Katarina finally slipped out before dawn to shower and change for the next work day.

The following week was a stressful period of conflicting emotions, starting with the pleasurable memories of that first night together. Working together and being forced to display only a professional demeanor while keeping Robbie in the dark about their relationship, which was consummated every night, created a certain level of stress between them.

At the end of the first week, the tension became too much for Katarina, and just before her father left for the night, she took him aside into the office.

"Dad…Craig and I have been sleeping together for the past week. I wanted to tell you because I am happier than I have ever been before."

Robbie jumped to his feet and strode out of the office, into the restaurant, shaking his head.

"Craig, git your ass into the office, now!" He turned on his heel and stormed out.

Craig edged into the office, fearing what was about to go down, but determined to deal with the consequences.

"So I hear you've been screwing my daughter." Robbie sat in the big office chair as Katarina cowered behind him.

"Yes, sir. Actually, I have actually been making love to your daughter. Because I do love her, even though I haven't yet made that declaration to her."

Robbie, who had been sitting there with murder in his eyes, suddenly smiled.

"I know. I've known since Monday. You cannot fool a father. What I've seen in my daughter's eyes and her body language toward you, and yours toward her, leaves me no doubt that you two were meant to be together. You both have my blessing, so you don't need to walk on eggshells anymore."

On shaky legs, Craig walked to a chair and sat. "So everything is cool?"

"Yes."

Katarina walked over behind Craig's chair. She bent down and wrapped both her arms around his neck.

"And I love him, Dad."

Despite the comfortable rapport between those present, time was to belie that dramatically.

Several idyllic months later, Katarina was to surprise both Craig and her father with a sudden announcement that she was heading to southern California to attend a college to study urban design and planning in order to start a career.

Both men tried unsuccessfully to talk her out of it, arguing that the college in town was as good as any.

Two days later, early in the morning, they both waved goodbye as her car, loaded with all the things she thought she would need for the first year of a two-year course, disappeared into the distance.

Craig was devastated, unable to comprehend why she would have this sudden change of mind and heart. Although they did discuss it many times, her mind was obviously made up and nothing he said could dissuade her from her chosen course. She even made him promise her that he would stay on with her father until she returned. In return, she promised to video-call him every day to assure him of her progress.

As they watched Katarina's car crest the hump in the Las Olas Bridge, Craig turned to Robbie and asked, "Did you foresee this happening?"

"No, not at all. I knew that she was mulling over several courses of action, but to suddenly pack up and leave is something I don't understand."

"She will be all right, won't she?"

"Oh, sure, she's a level headed girl; hard working, loyal and whip smart; she'll be fine."

Craig was understandably concerned about the possibility of losing the woman he loved to someone in California. "I just don't understand why she would not want me to come with her."

"I know the answer to that one, because she told me she wanted you to stay and help me here. You've become quite indispensible to me. And, I suppose, she wanted to be able to concentrate her entire attention on her studies; you are quite a distraction to her, you know."

Craig laughed, "Yes, I suppose I am."

"So what is this urban design and planning, anyway?"

"Actually, I think it would be a good course to take. It's laying out cities and towns, you know, allowing for parks, public buildings, recreational facilities, transportation and infrastructure. From what I have seen of the aliens' obviously advanced technology, and their apparent willingness to help us, it might very well be a growth industry."

"You could be right." Robbie allowed.

That evening, the first of Katarina's promised video-calls came in and Craig and Robbie took it in the office. Her beamingly happy and excited face appeared before them. She had made it to Mobile, Alabama on the first day of her four-day trip across the country, and she was looking forward to a nice meal and a good night's sleep. She apologized for the rushed departure but knew that if she had stayed any longer, they might have talked her out of going. She asked and was assured that everything was going well at the restaurant, and allowed that she missed them already. After an appropriate interval, Robbie left the office to allow Craig and his daughter to have their romantic conversation in private. It took quite a while, even after only one day.

The next day, it was business as usual. Robbie had hired on a new girl to take on Katarina's duties and she seemed to be working out quite nicely. She was quiet, efficient and competent. Craig went through his normal routine and was looking forward to the video call from Katarina.

By seven it still had not come in, and at eight he went into the office looking for Robbie. He found him sitting at his desk, head down in his arms on the desktop, and sobbing quietly. He raised his head as Craig came in and he was shocked to see tears flowing freely from Robbie's eyes.

"What has happened?" he asked urgently.

"I've just had a call from the Texas State Patrol. They told me that they have found Katarina's car, out of gas and stripped of anything of value, on a side road off the interstate just outside Dallas. They have not found Katarina or any sign of her."

"What!"

"They said that they would call as soon as they had any further news, good or bad. They don't know what happened."

Without another word, Craig took a seat next to Robbie and could feel the tears beginning to prick at his eyes. '*This can't be happening,*' he thought, but realized that it could.

Katarina was standing beside Charlie on the bridge of the alien flagship, watching the deception play out from a microscopic hidden video camera in the office. Her heart went out to Craig and Robbie in their suffering, but it was tempered by the sense of duty which was strong in her.

"In your twenty five years on Earth since your birth," Charlie said. "I know you have had a difficult time dealing with knowing your mother was an alien who was placed on Earth to produce a baby. One of the first alien women to produce a viable baby, she refused to come back until you were of an age to understand the agenda she had set for you. I hope you will remember the promise you made to her when she revealed the truth to you." He put an arm around her shoulders and tried to comfort her.

"Yes, I do remember. And you know that I am committed to this program. I just want to thank you for allowing me to choose my own partner. I do think that I chose well. He is a good man."

"Your pregnancy has been confirmed by our doctors, I take it." Charlie said.

"Yes. Confirmed and double-checked. A normal baby."

"He will be all right. It is better that he doesn't know." Charlie tried to console her. "You do realize, don't you, that this duty you have performed is the beginning of the future for our species—the only way we can survive."

Katarina turned to him with tears in her eyes. "I know exactly what this means and what my duty is," she whispered, "or I wouldn't have volunteered for the assignment in the first place. And granted, that while it was a pleasant assignment, it hurts badly. I still have feelings for him."

Charlie whispered, "I know what you must be feeling, but I think it would be better if you returned to your quarters and not prolong the suffering. You are relieved of all duties until the baby is born, and then your only duty will be to the welfare of yourself and of that child."

"Thank you, sir." She turned and walked off the bridge, toward the VIP accommodations.

Charlie watched her go with sadness in his heart, wishing there was another way to accomplish the mission, but knowing there wasn't.

PART 3

The first year went smooth, considering the inconceivable notion that the earth's population was being asked to accept. The first few months saw 90 percent of the earth's nuclear, natural gas, oil-fired and coal-burning power plants replaced by the alien power cell plants.

The process was simple. A box-car-sized power cell would be transported by the aliens to a prepared concrete pad, and the electrical connections to the power grid would be made. A few seconds' blackout would occur during the switchover and the new system would immediately take over the needs of the entire grid. No fence or guards were necessary since the power cell, like the ships and the aliens themselves, were invulnerable to any human weapon, and were self-contained and maintenance-free. It was like a hundred-year storage battery—it pumped out the power no matter what.

As soon as the power cell was in place, demolition crews would demolish the old power plants, which were an eyesore, and leave beautiful park land in its place, covered with vine-covered trellises.

The workers at the power plants, as well as the oil, natural gas and coal industries, who had been displaced by the virtual shutdown of their professions, all went into a selective training program in fields that the aliens said would not be affected by the changeover. They retained their normal rate of pay during training. Since the owners of the power plants didn't have to spend money on fuel, the consumers of that power saw a sharp decrease in the cost of their energy requirements.

The sailors on the oil tankers that had been dry docked due to the decreased demand for oil worldwide were also being compensated for their displacement, trained in other fields, or helped with their job search while still being paid at their normal rate, with full benefits included.

The soldiers, sailors, and airmen who found themselves crowded onto overflowing military bases, and the governments who found themselves with a glut of highly trained killers on-hand, did present a problem for a while. The officials who woke up soonest and employed the majority of these men in the various sectors of law enforcement and security, soon found themselves with sharply decreased crime statistics. The sudden increase in apprehensions and convictions fueled an increase in the number of prisons needed, which led to increased hiring of correction officers. The other former military personnel were offered training in other lines of work of their own choosing, at the government's expense and with full pay.

That first year seemed to be a win-win situation for everyone. There appeared to be peace in the world, with even the worst trouble spots around the globe settling into a cease-fire.

Even Amos, impressed with the visitors' plans, put his Barrett away and decided to wait and see what the aliens' plan would bring.

As the year wore on and the fossil fuel and nuclear power plants were eliminated from the earth, the visitors dropped another bombshell. They said that all Hover cars, automobiles, trucks, buses, trains, planes, boats, ships, and submarines—anything that was powered by fossil fuels or nuclear energy—could be retrofitted with smaller versions of the power cells which now supplied electricity to most of the world. Those that were worth saving would be, and the rest would be scrapped and replaced with new ones.

At this announcement, the world sat up and listened. And when they were told it would be free to install, and that they would never have to spend money on fuel ever again, they listened with even greater intensity. Naturally, the oil-producing nations and companies were not happy with this revelation.

During the latter part of that first year, the aliens introduced another innovation—the garbage disposal. No, not like the one in your kitchen sink, but one of the hundreds of thousands of units which would be transported to every landfill on Earth to recycle everything that had been buried. It would be dug up again, and along with everything that new refuse coming into the landfill, would be fed into the garbage disposal. And through the aliens' knowledge of molecular chemistry, it would then be transformed into useable raw materials. When anything was broken down into its atomic state, it could be reassembled into anything—steel, gold, plastics, food, or fertilizers. Even human waste would be processed on the atomic level.

Another problem plaguing the various countries of the world was addressed during the first year. This was the decaying state of the infrastructure of the many countries around the world, who for many decades, if not centuries, had ostensibly spent a disproportionate amount of money on national defense, while simply lining the pockets of defense contractors and lobbyists who gouged their governments at every turn. This resulted in the people who were actually paying the taxes—that is, the working class—were seeing less and less return for their money as budget overseers took a larger and larger share of the taxes for themselves.

Naturally, bridges, tunnels, roads, buildings, the power grid, railroad tracks, water and sewerage systems, broke down with regularity due to lack of maintenance.

A plan was enacted to utilize all the men and women who were sitting around and due to the shutdown of various industries, to work with the Army Corp of Engineers to fix, renovate, or replace all the infrastructure projects that had been pushed to the back-burner for far too long. As soon as the other countries of the world saw what America—finally rising out of its stupor—was doing, they decided to follow suit. All across the world, inadequate systems that for decades had become normal—such as flooded streets and neighborhoods, frequent electric and water outages, collapsing bridges, potholed roads, and lack of adequate food, clean water, public services, and basic amenities—were now addressed, and as a result, the standard of living was raised at an unbelievable rate. Even the vocal skeptics of the aliens' plan had to admit that finally things were getting better rather than worse.

At the end of the first year, in which the human race had experienced a turmoil that had never been seen before, Charlie decided to convene another United Nations meeting, one which, in the future, would be called the Annual State of the Earth Address. It would be attended by the heads of every country, and was to be broadcast simultaneously on every TV channel, radio station, and on the Internet.

YEAR 2

PART 1

Charlie once again, as he had the year before, materialized out of thin air behind the podium at the front of the United Nations Assembly.

He removed his helmet. "Welcome to you all. Once again, the chosen, at least for the most part, leaders of the world are assembled in one place. I thank every one of you for taking the time to attend this meeting and voting as you see fit for the future of your planet. This meeting will consist of two parts. In the first part, I will deliver a report, verbally and in both printed and electronic form, informing you of the results of the measures to contain the planet's pollution, which we initiated together one year ago. Feel free to distribute this report to whomever you desire, because I am certain that you, and they, will find it enlightening and encouraging."

"In the second part, I will introduce to you those things that we have determined would be appropriate to occur, with your approval, in the coming year—our second since we revealed our presence to you. You will see before you the same red, yellow, and green buttons as were there at our last meeting. They will be used for the same purpose as they were before, and again, the vote has to be unanimous, because since this is a worldwide effort, if we do not all agree to a certain proposal, it won't be implemented."

Charlie turned and gestured to an empty spot, where a one-hundred-foot electronic screen then materialized in mid-air. It began to fill with numbers and shapes, looking like an old-fashioned PowerPoint presentation.

He turned back to his audience with a smile. "I am now pleased to tell you that all the initiatives we put in place last year have borne fruit, and in a most spectacular way. Because of the withdrawal of foreign troops from all countries around the world, the large scale attacks we have come to expect from certain regions of the world have now been eliminated. We have had to intervene in only three major incidents in the past year. The first was when certain elements of ISIS decided in their stupidity to try to retake Tikrit. While they were assembling in the desert, they found that their vehicles, weapons, ammunition, food, water, and even their clothes had been transported to one of our ships, and they were left to wander around the desert in their skivvies. They were subsequently rounded up by the Syrian militia and imprisoned.

"The second involved the Taliban, when they tried to build yet another car bomb. They found that the car, their explosives, weapons, and bomb-making equipment had disappeared, transported to one of our ships. That they were surrounded by Afghan police meant a quick trip to lockup.

"The third was the well-publicized incident involving the meeting of the top echelon of Al-Qaeda, when they found themselves surrounded by police and shipped off to jail. The press had a field day with that one. There have also been several minor incidents from all around the world, but these have all been stopped, and the participants have been jailed."

Charlie indicated the figures on the screen behind him. "As you can see from the latest figures, the elimination of nearly one hundred percent of the power plants that were replaced by the power cells we installed has already had a remarkable effect on the health of the planet. There has been a ninety-four percent reduction in worldwide atmospheric pollution. In China, and other places that haven't seen blue skies for decades, are starting to see clear, sunny days with breathable air. The earth will never again need to be powered by fossil or nuclear fueled plants, and that in itself should keep pollution at minimal levels. We have also located and transported off the earth, all spent nuclear fuel rods and other nuclear waste, and consigned it to be destroyed in outer space, relieving the threat of radioactive contamination of ground water, on which the majority of the world's population depends for their drinking water.

"As of the end of the year, about forty-four percent of your vehicles—land, sea, and air—have been converted to the smaller power cells by retrained workers around the world, and the effort is continuing. Those vehicles considered too old for the conversion are being replaced by new vehicles, at no charge. Even those homes that are dependent on natural gas are being converted to the free electricity now being generated by the power cells, and the installation is at no cost to the homeowner."

Charlie took a sip of water from the glass that had appeared on the podium, as if by magic.

"Mainly due to the lack of need for soldiers, there has been an influx of highly trained security personnel and police officers in every country across the world, resulting in crime statistics being down across the board. Murders have been reduced by eighty-nine percent, robberies and break-ins by ninety-three percent, sex crimes by seventy-seven percent, and drug-related crimes by ninety-eight percent. This is good, of course, but not good enough. We can do better, especially concerning crimes against women and children."

Charlie placed his hands on the podium and leaned forward.

"I have received favorable reports from all corners of the globe to the effect that the people of the earth are pleased with the progress we have made so far, and wish to carry on with the plans we have implemented. There has been an exponential rise in the earning capacity and quality of life across the board, even among those laid off by the curtailing of certain industries. They have, with their free training, been able to find more interesting and better-paying jobs with the help of our consultants.

"Understandably, some of the company owners who saw their industry become extinct are upset at their loss of income. However, the less than one percent of the population who have for so long enjoyed the luxuries of life by exploiting the general public will simply have to learn to live with less, or find another legal way to increase their income. No longer will the poor and middle class be denied the opportunity to advance themselves because they were struggling under the thumbs of the rich. My heart does not bleed for those rich people who have for years exploited people less fortunate, less educated, or less dishonest than they are. While there are wealthy people in the world who want nothing more than to see their fellow man succeed in the world, there are far too many more who will exploit everyone, even their own grandmother, if given the chance, and whose only allegiance is to money."

He waited for challenges to this statement, but there were none.

"I feel we have come a long way in only one year. The virtual elimination of war, the extra security of an increased police force, the almost total elimination of pollution, and the raising of living standards for ninety-eight percent of the world's population is cause for celebration. The most important for me, however, is the increased awareness from the general populace that there is a better world right here, if only we accept each other as equals and pull together instead of pulling apart and trying to compete with your fellow man, while feeling only hatred and resentment for each other. If we have reached into the psyche of only a few people around the world, and shown them that there is a better way, we have achieved our goal for this year, and we are therefore prepared to go ahead with our plans for the second year, with the approval of all who are gathered here today.

"Reflecting on the successes of this past year, if we pull together and apply ourselves to the task, we can ensure that this next year will be just as successful."

Paul Johnson supposed it was inevitable that something like this would happen to him, since he was a stranger in these parts, and at times overwhelmed by circumstances.

On this day, he had finished a delayed trip to the grocery store to resupply his larder with all the commodities that ensured he kept up the strength to keep breathing. He packed the frozen items into a sealed cooler of dry ice, for his cabin was far off the beaten track deep into the backwoods of the Appalachian Mountains. Due to the infusion of essentials, he was looking forward to another couple weeks of solitude. It seemed to him that he always worked better at his fiction writing profession when he was not subject to the distractions of civilization, and soothed by the hushed sounds of nature.

As usual, Paul had turned off the main two-lane road leading out of town, onto a gravel street that the government called a forest service *road*. It had been not that long ago that he had been intimidated by the twisting, narrow road the first time he traversed it. But, having travelled it for a few months now, he had gotten used to it.

About five miles up this road, he was negotiating the roughest section of this so-called road—which was off-camber, winding, with a fifty-foot cliff to the right, and a fifty-foot drop off into a steep gully to the left—when he saw a flash of red in his peripheral.

He jammed on the brakes, got out and inched back to the source of the color.

A red Jeep with a black canvas top had slid off the road, and had only been stopped from the fifty-foot plunge into the gully by a tree, which was now jammed against the driver's side door. The passenger side door was wide open, and even from the road ten feet above he could make out a smudge of blood on the driver's side window. Of much more concern, though, was the puddle of blood on the passenger seat.

Paul shouted, "Hello! Is anyone around?"

No answer.

He picked down the steep slope and crept up to the vehicle, afraid of what he might find inside.

The Jeep was empty, but Paul found a fresh blood trail leading to an hiking trail across the road. He hesitated, but eventually decided to follow the blood trail into the forest to see if he could help whoever was out there.

He hiked the ever increasingly dense foliage, aware that a black cloud had formed overhead, making the whole scene gloomy, and it was turning what was an already dismal situation into a questionable quest.

After only a couple hundred yards, his mind started reminding him of all the stories he had heard about rattlesnakes, coyotes, mountain lions, and black bears, and he had thoughts of turning back and calling the police. He even took out his cell phone. But being a long way from any cell towers way, there was no signal.

Paul was about to turn around and go back to his truck, when he heard whimpering, and he struggled forward a few more yards despite his trepidation. When he saw a form propped against a tree only a few yards further down the trail, he dug deep and summoned the courage to proceed.

It was a girl. Although, at his age, any woman under fifty was a girl. She was obviously in a great deal of pain. As he approached, he saw that the bone in her upper arm was sticking out of her skin, and blood was pouring from the wound.

Paul knelt beside her and tried to comfort her. He wondered if he should try to take her to a hospital, or if he should he get her comfortable, then go get help. If he left her, he feared he would return to a corpse. So he decided to try to get her to his truck and take her to the hospital at the bottom of the hill.

"Greg?" she slurred.

"No, I'm not Greg. But I'm going to get you to the hospital."

Paul tore part of a shirt and used it as a tourniquet to apply to her arm, which stopped most of the bleeding, while using the rest of the shirt for a sling. He secured her lower arm to her waist by wrapping his belt around her makeshift sling.

"I'm not going anywhere without Greg. He has all the money."

"Lady, right now I have only two choices. Either I can take you with me to the hospital, or I can leave you here while I go get help. It is entirely your choice. I don't know who or where Greg is, or even if he is coming back, but you have already lost a lot of blood, and if I don't get you to a doctor soon, you are going to bleed out, and possibly die right here."

Her strident attitude seemed to collapse, and she allowed him to assist her in standing. Together they started to hobble back towards his truck.

It took a while to make the short trip to his truck, with her getting weaker with each step, but they finally made it to the truck, her breathing ragged. Paul placed her in the passenger seat, strapped her in.

The nightmare trip down the mountain was accentuated by high-pitched screams accompanied by whimpering. His heart went out to her, and as he sped along the rutted gravel road, her agony remained in the forefront of his mind.

In a town of only eighteen hundred people, the regional hospital was quiet on that Monday evening. They even had to wake up the doctor on-call, who had been snoozing in the break room. But shortly after Paul arrived, the girl was rushed to the operating room.

Paul finally got a phone signal and called 911 and explained the situation to the operator. The police were there within five minutes, and after assessing the situation, asked him to come to the police station to fill out a report.

"Where exactly did you find her?"

He explained where the road to his cabin started, and they finally located on a map the trail where he had found the girl. A few calls on the radio seemed to calm them since there was only one way in and out of that trail. They would send a search party into the woods from each end, and assuming he had not left the trail, were certain they would locate the elusive Greg.

After taking all the pertinent information, the sergeant in charge of the investigation thanked Paul profusely, lent him a police T-shirt, and after a couple hours, finally allowed him to go home. Paul contemplated stopping at the hospital to see the girl on the off-chance that she would be so grateful she would want to see him again after she was released from the hospital. But then reality set in. Why would a beautiful young woman want to associate with an old fart like him?

Paul headed for home, back to his lonely old cabin in the woods. He was apprehensive as he passed the red Jeep still stuck against the tree, but all seemed quiet, and he finally reached home hours after he'd planned. Thank goodness the dry ice in the cooler had done its job and kept his frozen purchases cold enough to survive.

After a quick dinner, he got to bed at his normal time and slept soundly. Although, he did have a few sensual thoughts about the young lady he had rescued, and how grateful she might have been toward her rescuer.

He was awakened early the next morning by banging on his front door. In his robe, he reluctantly allowed that same sergeant from the night before into his sanctuary, amazed that the policeman had been able to find his well-hidden location, a long way away from the single lane gravel road leading to his cabin. Over coffee, the sergeant explained to him the facts of the case they were working on.

"We want to thank you for all you did yesterday, and to let you know the outcome. After a coordinated search, we did find Greg about a quarter-mile from the other end of the trail. He was dead from a fractured skull, and even the medical examiner was amazed that he made it that far. He had the thirty thousand dollars on his person. So thanks to you, we can now close the case." With heartfelt thanks, the officer shook Paul's hand.

Paul stood there, bewildered. "What thirty thousand dollars are you talking about?"

"Why, the money they stole from the bank in town. They were both bank robbers."

So much for my dreams.

Two weeks later, early morning, Paul heard the sound of tires on gravel, an unusual sound given the distance his cabin was from the road. He listened intently as the vehicle approached and came to a stop outside his front door.

Paul removed his S&W 38 revolver from its hidden compartment in the bedroom, before moving to the back door. As he stepped onto the wraparound deck surrounding the house, he heard the front doorbell chime. He crept along the side deck and snuck up behind the person at the front door, keeping the gun hidden behind his back.

Paul faltered when he saw her back, but as she turned away from the door in a display of frustration, a spark of recognition flared. Standing before him was the girl he had rescued, her arm in a sling.

The cop said she was a criminal, so why isn't she in jail? Did she escape, or make bail? Is she here to hurt me?

"Can I help you?" he said.

She plastered a smile upon her beautiful face as she completed the quarter rotation. For some reason, that smile made him relax. But not enough that he returned her smile.

"Hi, Paul. I'm Melanie, and I wanted to come up here to thank you properly for saving my life. The sheriff gave me your name and address."

To say that he was somewhat taken aback would be the understatement of the year.

"W-why don't we go in back and, uh, sit a while?"

He guided her to the table and two chairs on the back deck overlooking the forest and white mountain laurel, and in the background, mountains of varying shades of blue. Apart from its isolation, that view was one of the main reasons he had chosen this cabin.

He sat, still wary of her, but she said she preferred to remain standing.

"So Melanie, why don't you tell me what happened. It must have been quite an ordeal for you."

"First of all, I can guess what the sergeant told you about me when he came to see you a couple weeks ago, and I want you to know that I had no part in the bank robbery. Greg told me he needed to make a withdrawal from the bank, but I had no idea that he meant robbing it. I was horrified. Greg had to physically drag me out of the bank and force me into the car. Afterwards, they decided not to charge and subsequently released me due to the witness statements and the information that the sheriff got from the aliens confirming that I had no hand in what was happening. I don't remember very much between the crash and waking up in the hospital, but when the sheriff found out who I was, he gave me all the details about what you had done for me, and I decided to reward you. So here I am." She finally pulled up a chair and sat.

"And who are you, exactly?"

"My name is Melanie DeAngelo," she said, with expectation of recognition.

But Paul sat there with a blank expression.

"I am the only child of Joe DeAngelo, the mayor of Las Vegas."

Paul's made an O shape with his lips, but said nothing.

"Anyway, after the sheriff contacted my father and received a thorough tongue lashing from him, and since the bank was reluctant to press charges against me since they got their money back, they had little choice but to release me on my own recognizance. The hospital was happy because I paid their bill in full."

"Wow! You've had quite an adventure, haven't you?"

"Yes, I have. And now, since you saved my life, it's time for your reward. You can have anything you want—my money, my body, my gratitude, or anything else you desire. The only question is, what do you want?"

"Does your arm still hurt?"

"Not as much as it did." She removed the sling and lifted her arm over her short-cropped black hair and placed it on the table.

Paul could see no indication of a break.

She stood and started undoing the front of her shirt. It took only a few buttons to prove that she wore no bra, revealing her well-endowed breasts. She slid the shirt onto the floor and placed her hands on her shapely hips.

Paul gawked at the sight before him. How could this beautiful young sexy woman want him?

"I-I don't think…"

"Why not? Is it lack of ability, or lack of desire? You're not gay, are you?"

"No, I am not gay. But I am old enough to be your father."

"That doesn't matter to me. I am here to reward you, not marry you." She kicked off her flip-flops, undid the button and zipper on her short shorts, and slid them gracefully down to her ankles, then stepped out of them.

No underwear, either. He felt his desire between his legs. *She came prepared.*

She, too, noticed the growing lump in his trousers, and moved closer. She reached down and started unbuttoning his shirt, until he stopped her.

He stood and noticed he was only a couple inches taller than she was. He finished with the buttons and removed his shirt, and then his loafers, pants, and briefs, and welcomed her into his arms as she snuggled against him.

After a brief moment, he took her by the hand and led her into the master bedroom. She followed.

Normally asleep by ten, and woke around five each morning, Paul was surprised to find the sun high in the sky when he stirred the next morning.

Not surprising, given the workout she gave me. A lecherous grin formed.

For an old man, he had performed well.

Paul rolled over in bed and threw an arm to her side of the bed, but found only empty space. He looked across and noticed the indentation on her pillow, proving that last night was not just a wicked dream. Realizing he was ravenous, he stood and threw on his robe and went looking for her and for breakfast, not necessarily in that order.

She was nowhere to be found. He checked the other bedroom and both bathrooms before concluding that she wasn't there.

He noted that her shirt, short shorts and flip-flops were still on the floor, and her sling was still on the table.

She must be outside enjoying the morning sunshine. After all, the cabin's isolation would have encouraged her to wander around outside naked without any chance of embarrassment.

Paul stepped through the back door, onto the porch, expecting to see her lounging on the cushioned swing with its magnificent view of the valley, but she wasn't there. He then walked around the wraparound porch until he reached the front of the cabin, and stopped dead in his tracks.

Her car was gone.

She must have had a change of clothes in the car.

He stood there for a while before he noticed the anomaly of the scene. His gravel parking area showed the tracks that her car had made when she arrived, and even the indentations of her car being parked overnight. But there were no tracks leading away from her parking spot.

After breakfast, Paul drove into town and went to the sheriff's office. When he walked in, he was ushered into the back office, where the sheriff confronted him.

"Do you know where the woman calling herself Melanie DeAngelo is?" the sheriff said.

"Well, she was at my place last night, but she was gone this morning."

The sheriff appeared astounded. "What was she doing there?"

"Thanking me for saving her life. After all, you did give her my name and address."

"I didn't give her Jack shit. If I had my way, she'd still be sitting in my jail cell. But she has disappeared, and so has every piece of evidence against her. In fact, her whole file is gone."

"Yes, I know she's gone. But the funny thing is, her car is gone, too, but it didn't leave any tracks when she left my cabin."

"There's something screwy about this whole situation. When I did what I should have done in the first place and sent the lineup photos to Mayor DeAngelo in Las Vegas, he told me that she was definitely *not* his daughter. When we searched every database we could find, her fingerprints could not be identified. That, of course, is not proof of a crime. She just may not be in the system. But the aliens' database was clear about who she was. I'm beginning to suspect they know more about this than they're letting on."

"So your pregnancy has been confirmed?"

Charlie was standing next to Melanie in his ready room, watching the drama unfolding in the sheriff's office.

"Yes, it has," she replied. "And I must say that this has been one of my more pleasant assignments. For an old man, he was surprisingly virile and inventive, but gentle at the same time. The only bad part of the whole situation is that I wish we could let all the fathers know how they're helping us, and why. I will not forget Paul."

"That is only one of the parts of this program that bothers me, and it is something I intend to bring up with the Council of the Continuum at the next meeting. But for now, congratulations on a job well-done. And as with all the mothers-to-be, you are relieved of all duties except to look after yourself and your baby, before and after birth."

Melanie retired to her VIP cabin, a welcomed change from the military barracks where she normally slept. She turned on the sixty-inch video screen and tuned in to the channel following Paul and the sheriff through the microscopic spy camera which could be set up and retrieved by a transporter beam, to any place on Earth.

Although she appeared to be in her early twenties, by earth standards, Melanie was two hundred years old, having been born on the home world, and immediately recruited for this mission. She finally admitted to herself that there were some aspects of this mission that were not so pleasant.

She gazed at the image of Paul, and with a heavy heart, realized that she would probably never see him again. And for some reason, that bothered her.

With reluctance, she finally switched off the monitor to try to regenerate some of the rest she had missed the night before.

PART 2

Back at the UN, Charlie continued, "This coming year, we are going to concentrate our efforts on something that has plagued the human population from your earliest beginnings. And that is the problem of the health of the world's population, which is abysmal, at best, at the moment. The current healthcare systems in place around the world allow the wealthy all the healthcare they can afford, whether they need it or not, and withhold healthcare from those who desperately need it if they cannot afford to pay for it. This is an arcane system that is going to stop immediately."

He paused and noted that certain sectors of his audience were smiling, knowing that help was on the way, and the rest were frowning, for they knew from where that help was going to come.

"There is an extremely important point that I know will disturb you all. We have deliberately chosen not to reveal it until now, because we were afraid that some people might get the notion that Big Brother has been watching you. But we have decided to reveal the extent to which we have followed your planet up to this point.

We have aboard each of our ships a very sophisticated computer system, far in advance of anything on Earth, which has identified and is tracking every human being on planet Earth through their DNA. And utilizing these machines, we can tell exactly where you are, what you are doing, your state of health, and it gives us a good idea of what you plan on doing in the near future."

There were gasps of disapproval from almost all sections of the audience, and shouts of protest from those who had the most to lose from the surveillance. Charlie allowed the outrage to continue for a while, before holding his hands up for silence.

"The reason we have developed this system of surveillance is to identify the healthcare issues that each individual has in order to treat them effectively. Over the many years of our existence, we have identified and developed cures for every disease that would conceivably harm a human being. These cures will be made available to the general public shortly, free of charge. Everything from the common cold to cancer and heart disease can and will be eradicated."

Charlie leaned back from the podium and surveyed the gathering before him. He smiled at their consternation.

"That will mean there will no longer be a need for any research labs or pharmaceutical companies, except as manufacturing plants for the new drugs that everyone will need. I realize that this will cause a great deal of upheaval amongst those who consider themselves above the general riffraff below them, but they will have to learn to live with it. I promise you that since we will provide you with all the formulas, a solution is coming.

"During this year, we will also tackle the lack of food for the starving millions in many parts of the world. As most intelligent people know, it is not the lack of food and water that plagues the starving population, but lack of equitable distribution. There is plenty of food in the world for everybody. There are even places where certain governments pay farmers *not* to grow food, or will even destroy it in order for the price of this commodity to be kept artificially high. I have never been able to understand this phenomenon. But then, I am not a white-collar thief consumed by greed."

Charlie looked across the room, pausing at the leaders of the first-world nations.

"By utilizing the power cells and the garbage disposals which we have placed in under-developed countries, we intend to make up for any shortfall caused by discriminatory food distribution. Using our transporters, we can remove food from a region with a surplus, and deliver it to a region with a deficit, and it will all be free. We can also do the same with water, so that once again the Sahara Desert, and other arid regions, will bloom with grass, flowers, and trees. No more will government interference or greedy middlemen be allowed to cause the starvation of millions of people whose only crime was to be born in the wrong place."

He paused to collect himself, his emotions rising.

"This might cause some hardships, but as I see it, starvation is the ultimate hardship, and I have no sympathy for anyone who might lose a few bucks."

A slow clapping caught everyone's attention, and Charlie was not surprised to see the self-proclaimed king of one of the impoverished nations of Africa stand up and applaud louder and louder. The king was soon joined by others of the same persuasion, until the noise rose to a crescendo. Soon, all had joined in the tumult, except a few of the developed nations who felt that they would be left holding the shitty end of the stick.

They were right, for the excesses of the wealthy, and the power struggles of many governments, were soon going to come to an end, and not in a way anyone saw coming.

PART 3

Charlie announced a thirty-minute break and then faded from view. The representatives for the world leaders were allowed to obtain food and drink for their parties.

The huge screen upon which the statistics had been displayed slowly changed, and was now showing colorful scenes of the various parts of the earth that had been the most affected by the initiatives undertaken the year before. The numerous before-and-after pictures flashed upon that screen were awe-inspiring. Brilliant scenes taken at the worst trouble spots were compelling in their contrast. Even the photos of the planet taken from space showed a much brighter and clearer atmosphere. There was no doubt that, even in the short space of one year, the Earth was a healthier place.

After the promised thirty minutes had elapsed, Charlie materialized once again behind the lectern. He waited until he had been noticed by everyone.

"Thank you for allowing me to meet with my advisory panel. We have decided that the best way forward is to lay out for you the whole ten-year plan so you will not be in the dark about what will happen, with your consent. Just to be clear, none of what we propose will happen without your one-hundred-percent agreement. We are not here to dictate to you. Before moving on, I will answer any questions you have for me."

The president of the United States, Sylvia Han-Chin, stood.

Even Boris Chevsonenko, Russia's president, remained seated, grinning. *Let her take some criticism for a change.*

"Charlie, with your permission, I have a statement first, and then some questions."

He bowed. "By all means, continue, Madam President. I value your opinion, and I am anxious to hear what you have to say."

She glanced around and saw a mixture of faces staring back, some friendly, some not so much.

"First, I'd like to say how pleased the government and the people of the United States, and indeed, the world, are at the remarkable results that have been achieved by the power cells and garbage disposals that were installed over the past year. I was skeptical at first, as I am sure many people were, but the results have been unbelievable. If we achieve nothing else together, this change has given Earth a brand-new lease on life. And for that, I, and the people of earth, thank you."

Charlie bowed to acknowledge her appreciation.

"As to your new proposals, I wonder how much thought you've given to the closing of research facilities, and turning the pharmaceutical companies into pill factories. Do you realize how many people will be without a job, and how much investors stand to lose if this is allowed to happen?"

With a smirk, Charlie replied, "We have indeed, Madam President. And the answer to the first part of the dilemma is simply that, since we will give you all the answers and all the formulas, there will be no more need for research. The answer to the second part will be forthcoming in the revelations I have for you after the questions."

"But surely you must realize that humanity never agrees one hundred percent on anything. Certainly not on something that will take away their livelihood." Sylvia imagined the riots which would surely follow such an action.

"If my memory serves me correctly, it seems that last year, this assembly agreed one hundred percent to bringing home foreign troops. Or am I mistaken on that?"

"No, you are correct. But that was something that had to be done."

"Believe me, madam, this is also something that has to be done. Are there any other questions?"

Boris Chevsonenko heaved his bulk to a standing position as the diminutive Sylvia Han-Chin took her seat.

"Charlie...if I may call you that...if we agree to these proposals, what guarantees do we have that the burden will be shared equally?"

"By burden, I will assume that you mean an equal share of food and resources for every living person on the planet, regardless of wealth or position. And the answer to that is yes. Everyone will receive all the food they want, shelter, clothing and anything else they need, on an equitable basis, according to their personal desires. Right now, because of the replicators we have already installed—the so-called garbage disposals—if every person on this planet wanted a steak dinner, we could flood the Earth with steak. It would be the best steak you ever had, high in protein and low in fat, and it would not be bad for you, since the medicines we would give you would zero-out the bad content."

"So what you are saying is that you would not take from those that had a surplus," Boris said, "but simply enhance the supply of those who had a deficit?"

"Exactly. Those who have plenty will not have to give up anything, as long as it is not wasted. But those who have little or none will get all they need or desire." Charlie stepped back from the podium, while a bewildered Boris took his seat.

"This last revelation brings us to the discussions I had with my advisory panel during the break. This year, we intend to concentrate our efforts on the implementation of our plans for the manufacturing and distribution of the medicines the population needs, and the replication and distribution of the food and water to sustain those people in dire need. There is also a need to train or retrain a large number of people to be construction workers, which are needed around the world to build shelters for everyone without a home. And by shelter I mean a proper house, not a mud hut or a huge square of apartments, but a single-family home, a duplex, or a triplex. These people could easily come from the pharmaceutical or food industries, since a lot of the hard outdoor work will be eliminated by the technology we will be giving you."

He paused, for he felt sure that someone would point out that researchers were not the ideal people to be building houses. But no one commented.

"The houses would be built in a climate-controlled assembly building, and transported by one of our ships to where it was needed. A simple hookup to power, water, and sewerage, and the home would be ready for its new occupants."

From out of the darkness at the back of the assembly, someone shouted, "And who the hell is going to pay for all those homes?"

Charlie smiled. "I am so glad you asked me that. The short answer is, nobody. The people who get their new house would move in, get a certificate of ownership, and start living there. The people who build them would be paid by the company who employed them, and the materials would be free since they came from our replicator. Since there is no more war to spend money on, the com-panies would be paid per unit by the government, out of those savings. Naturally, this situation, which seems untenable, will only last for this coming year."

"What we intend to address next year are the three things that cause ninety-nine-point-nine percent of the misery on this planet, and has for thousands of years. They are money, national borders, and religion."

A different heckler shouted, "And what do you intend to do about them?"

Charlie's smile was even bigger this time. "Eliminate them!"

Stunned silence. And then everyone started shouting questions and comments at once, the crescendo of angry noise rising to ear-splitting levels. At the front of the room, Charlie stood surveying the scene before him, allowing everyone to shout themselves hoarse.

Silence slowly descended upon the chamber as the people realized that their protests had no effect on Charlie, and he allowed a small smile.

"This year, we will be working with all the governments of the world, all the banks, the stock markets, the mortgage companies, the insurance industry, and many billionaires and multi-millionaires around the world to determine the most efficient way to bring about changing a debt-laden world into a world without currency.

"While even I will admit that it won't be easy, will require an extensive amount of retraining, and may cause many hardships for some in the short-term, it is possible to achieve, and it is the equitable thing to do. On every planet in the consortium, there is *no* form of compensation, and it is working out very well. We are allowing for a one-year transition period during year three, and we anticipate that by year four everyone will be settled into the new system. This is something which must be done, because for people to be truly, equal they must be equally poor."

A long silence followed.

All around the world, those who heard Charlie's words went into an almost instant panic. There were several schools of thought naturally; those who were broke and living hand to mouth looked optimistically forward to not having to worry about money anymore; those who were swimming in debt without any possibility of paying it all back and losing everything they had, endorsed the plan enthusiastically; and those who had tons of money and credit, wondered what would become of them, since most of them had no skills other than the accumulation of more wealth. This last group, the so-called one percent, naturally condemned any such notion. It was beyond their belief that any such proposal could even have been made.

But bigger shocks were just around the corner, as Charlie outlined the next step in the plan. He smiled benignly, knowing the shock they must all be feeling.

"The next problem, for that is what it is, happens to be the division of the Earth into large and small fiefdoms, each with their own set of rules, regulations and laws. This is going to stop at the start of Year Three with a simple stroke of the pen. All countries of the world will declare their borders open and eliminated and everyone on the face of the earth will be governed by one set of laws which will apply to everyone everywhere. Since there will be no more money, there will no longer be a set of rules specifically for the wealthy, as there is now, since there won't be any more wealthy people. The elimination of national borders will not signal a mass exodus of people from poorer countries to wealthy countries since no country will be wealthier than another, and where you are right now might offer more and better opportunity for work which has not been eliminated by all these changes."

This time, this particular heckler at least had the decency to stand up. "But why do you think that people would want to work if they are not getting paid for it?"

"But they will be getting paid for it, at least in kind. When they are getting their upgraded housing, all of their food - as much as they can eat, their transportation, their training and retraining, their entertainment, and all their energy for free, they are in fact getting paid, don't you think?" Charlie argued.

"Yes, I guess that's true. But what if some people work diligently and some just shirk off?"

"You forget that we can track each individual by their DNA. We know where you are and what you are doing, and if you are shirking off, you will suddenly find that the grocery store won't give you any food, and someone will turn up to evict you from your house and repossess your Hover car. People legitimately between jobs can apply for work and will retain their privileges, but if in fact you are engaged in illegal activities or just don't want to work, you can sleep in a ditch and starve to death, as far as we are concerned. Artists and other self employed people will be identified and evaluated, and if found legitimate, will also retain their privileges. We don't want to discriminate against anyone, but there are too many good people in the world to allow the few rotten apples to spoil it for everyone else."

Charlie waited for the next question, and seemed slightly disappointed when one didn't come. "You must also remember that this elimination of certain things that everyone has had to live with all their lives will also have psychological consequences. One of the first things that I touched on during the first meeting was the difficulty of changing the human mind, and attempting to eliminate prejudices against others for any reason. We now will have a situation where all other things being equal, one person chooses not to pull his weight. How long do you seriously think that this person would have any more good neighbors, serious friends, mere acquaintances, or even their own self esteem, once everyone found out that they were sponging off the work of others?"

Undaunted, he continued, "And now we come to the big one; the one that will cause the most people grief and the one responsible for more deaths over the centuries than any other cause—religion! By that I mean organized religion, and the multitude of charlatans out there. I want to put this in the simplest terms possible so there can be no misunderstandings."

His big hands clenched the sides of the lectern and he leaned forward aggressively, and addressed them sternly so there could be no mistaking his words.

"Basically, there is no God. There is no higher being, benign or otherwise, looking after the affairs of men. There were no legitimate religious leaders in history; there was only US, my people, and we were and are not Gods. Religion was started by US as an ill-conceived notion by a predecessor of mine; basically a failed attempt in which we were hoping to teach the people back then to live in peace, goodwill and harmony. All, and I do mean ALL of the so-called religious figures of history were men and women from my race of people, playing roles which were designed to educate mankind about their obligations to their fellow man."

For the first time, the gathering felt the emotion which had crept into his voice, "The words of peace that we brought to the world were perverted and twisted by humans to mean whatever the author of the propaganda wanted the people to hear. All religions are guilty of this, from the Spanish Inquisition to ISIS and everyone in between and even before that in Buddhism, Hinduism and Shintoism, and even in native religions of America, Australia and Africa. And let us not forget the Incas and the Aztecs, among others. Even today, certain religious leaders maintain huge edifices, expensively decorated and filled with treasures from the past, while their impoverished parishioners scratch the earth for their meager living, and are pressured into giving more to their church than many cannot afford."

Charlie became emotionally distressed, which no one had seen from him before.

"This is going to stop!" he screamed.

Then he paused and hung his head, gripping the lectern in a vice-like grip. When he finally raised his head, his face was distorted with anguish, and his eyes glistened with suppressed tears.

"All organized religion will immediately stop extorting money from their parishioners," Charlie said, his voice quavering, "discontinue the trappings of their meetings, and disband their organizations. The governments of the world should make plans to seize the ill-gotten gains of these big-time swindlers who prey on the weak and the gullible. The people will be allowed to retain their own feelings on the matter, but no organized meetings of any kind will be tolerated. We will even allow the churches, temples, mosques, and other religious sites to stand in mute testimony of man's gullible notions, but no organized services will be performed within their walls."

Sylvia Han-Chin jumped to her feet. "I must protest! I was born and raised Catholic, and I resent the implications you are making. We do not believe that we have been duped all these years."

"Unfortunately, madam, everything I've said is true. From the Inquisition to the Lutherans to the Protestants, to the IRA to the Nazi extermination of the Jews with the Roman Catholic Cardinal of Germany looking on, to the PLO, the Taliban, Al Qaeda, to ISIS, the tales of bloody slaughter are recorded faithfully in your own history books. I don't even have to leave Europe and the Middle East to prove my point. You will surely be able to see the message I'm conveying to you. As I said last year, changing the environment was easy. Changing the human psyche is going to be the hardest thing I have ever tried. But I have to try, because if I don't succeed, I will have no choice but to incinerate this whole planet."

Sylvia sat slowly, and stared with haunted eyes. She made a mental note to meet with Ben Williamson, her secretary of state, as soon as this farce was over.

Charlie seemed exhausted, which was, probably the most normal thing that had happened so far. He stood like a statue for a long time, before stepping back from his aggressive stance at the podium, his eyes roaming from side to side.

He shook his head. "And now, finally, it is time for the vote. Remember that today, all you are voting on is the proposal to rid the world of all the diseases that have plagued the planet from day one, and the implementation of the food and housing plan, as I outlined it earlier. Everything else will come next year. Please indicate your choices now."

Quickly at first, and then slower as the vote reached the developed countries, until finally all the lights were lit, and they were all green.

"Excellent," Charlie said. "Until next time we meet, I bid you farewell."

He faded out to thunderous applause.

Some hours later, after relating the stories about the powers Charlie possessed, Sylvia Han-Chin and Ben Williamson had ensconced themselves in a private office inside the UN Building. Both were depressed at the thought of the upcoming changes.

"So now what are we going to do?" Sylvia said.

Williamson stared into an empty space somewhere between the ceiling and the floor.

"Fuck if I know. How are we going to keep our power base if there is no money?"

They sat silent for a long time, sipping their drinks.

Sylvia lit another cigarette. "Perhaps it is high time to call on Amos's skills once again."

Ben was startled. He wasn't aware that Sylvia knew he shared her secrets. Apart from Amos and Sylvia, as far as he knew, he was the only living person that knew of Sylvia's involvement in the assassination of the president of the United States all those years ago, gleaned from the many intelligence reports he had received as director of the CIA, and an insight and fertile imagination which left him with only one conclusion.

He looked over at her, concern etched on his face, and saw a calm, determined woman looking back at him.

"Even Amos can't help us this time. Charlie can't be killed. He's indestructible." Ben said.

"Really? Obviously we know from all our reports that his ships can withstand any attacks on them. We have yet to destroy, or even damage, one of them. But we only have Charlie's word that he is indestructible. It seems to me that we ought to at least attempt to verify that what he says is actually true, don't you think? Amos is the person to take the initiative for me, providing I can convince him that this is as important as last time."

Ben sat back in contemplation. If it turned out that Charlie *was* destructible, there might be a way to save the Earth from destruction and chaos.

“Do you even know how to contact him?” Ben replied.

“I’ve had him on my payroll for the last thirty years. It’s time he made a contribution to the cause. Besides, I know him too well. He will do it for me. And if not, he will do it for America.”

Nothing more was said.

Ben slipped a case out of his inside coat pocket and fired up a Cuban cigar while Sylvia lit another cigarette. They refilled and clinked their glasses.

Amos would be receiving a request that he probably expected, but dreaded, and the world would be safe once again.

YEAR 3

PART 1

Much to everyone's surprise, politicians and their constituents alike, the transition from a for-profit society to a world without any form of currency went much smoother than anybody would have believed. The announcement from each country's government that from the start of Year Three and beyond, all forms of money would be worthless, brought about uneasiness about the worth of each individual, and an uncertainty about the viability of the future.

After an initial rush for food and other commodities, which left many local stores empty, people noticed that most stores, especially grocery stores, were being restocked overnight by the aliens.

Amos was not worried since his was an out-of-the-loop existence. No money just meant he would not have to make the monthly trek over to his hidden money box. This was a blessing since his old truck had not been converted over to one of the alien's power modules, and it was becoming increasingly difficult to find unleaded gas anywhere in the area.

He considered contacting Randy about getting one of the new Dodge four-by-four trucks he had seen on his fifty-inch flatscreen, with a power module. Randy was his one friend, outside the government, that knew who Amos was. Or at least, had been. Now he was just an old soldier, put out to pasture.

Randy owned a rundown auto repair shop some miles outside Blairsville, Georgia, and that was where Amos's truck was registered. Changing over to a new truck would have been child's play, but for some reason Amos felt a strong emotional attachment to the old rust bucket. Go figure.

In the end, Amos made sure Randy had plenty of unleaded gas for him whenever he came to town.

The second part about the elimination of borders didn't affect him since he didn't travel outside the U.S. The only thing that bothered him was that the memories of the wars he had fought in now seemed meaningless. The wars over territory or resources meant nothing, and Amos recalled all those faces vividly—the ones he had served with, and the ones he had seen only through his sniper scope. Not usually a man of emotion, he now felt sorrowful.

As for the third revelation, he was in a quandary since he had served with the armed forces against a bunch of religious fanatics in the Middle East. Amos was not religious, but admitted to anyone who would listen that there had been many times when he had muttered, *Oh, God, get me out of this and I'll come to church every Sunday from now on.*

He had gotten out of those situations, but he had reneged on those promises. His explanation had been, *I wouldn't want the roof of the church to fall down on anyone.*

Still, he had a bone to pick with organized religion, the excesses, the pedophilia, the secrets, the accumulation of wealth, and the concept of *God on Earth* rankled him no end. While the Pope might have been a good and honorable man, there was no end of cardinals and archbishops who believed that the poor were for exploiting. Amos didn't even want to think about televangelists—money-grubbing assholes with big mouths. Most of them wouldn't even make worthy targets for his Barrett.

That night he actually fell asleep in his easy chair in front of his TV, contemplating his plans, when news outlets worldwide directed everyone on Earth to specific web pages in their particular country upon which they could be identified and asked a few pages of questions about their needs and desires. The needs were fulfilled immediately, and the desires were handled as the resources became available. Even requests for retraining to a more desirable job were handled quickly.

People realized that the world would grind to a halt if they stopped working, and most of the population of the world went to work as they normally would, despite not being paid with money.

The world's homeless population disappeared overnight as empty homes and condominiums were given to them by governments, at the aliens' insistence.

Those countries whose population exceeded available housing units, were placed on the priority list for the alien-designed-and-built houses.

In remote places in Africa and Asia, societies tended to cluster around the power plants supplied by the visitors, so it became easier to build the assembly plants in which the workers would construct these houses in air-conditioned comfort. The construction of these houses provided employment for the local population, and the units would later be transported by the aliens' ships to an appropriate site for someone's new home.

It took a while for the aliens' assertions to sink in—that a moneyless society was not only possible, but ,preferable. But as people saw that they were not going to miss out on the things that they were used to and were even getting more than what they were used to getting, the radical idea of no money gained overwhelming popularity. People started to appreciate that they had no more financial worries, didn't have to come up with a mortgage or car payment, didn't have to pay back their student loans, their credit card bills, or any other financial obligation.

The other outstanding return for the world was the elimination of all the diseases that had plagued mankind. Not only could you be cured of anything, but it was free. You didn't even have to have an insurance policy to cover the cost.

Over the course of the year, many terminal patients would come to realize that they could start planning their life again since they were not going to die. At least, not in the foreseeable future. Naturally, the most serious cases were treated first by means of an extensive triage system. But as the year drew to a close, most of the patients in the world's hospitals were victims of accidents, or of the few crimes that were still being committed.

Crime took another blow to the chin since there was no way to profit from it. Gambling was another casualty, except for pleasure, and professional sports were played by those who were in it for the game and the glory, not for the money.

There were enormous numbers of millionaires and billionaires who decried this state of affairs since they had not been trained for anything else except screwing over their fellow man. Those with inherited wealth were forced to find a job to meet the requirements of the visitors' edict.

Surprisingly, the issue of national borders caused the least amount of problems. The countries with representatives at the UN assembly stayed in session until all the countries were in agreement to the laws of the world. All of the states within those countries were finally convinced that a uniform, worldwide set of laws pertaining to everyone was preferable to what was currently on the books.

The much anticipated mass migration across now-open borders never happened. The people in the lesser developed countries seemed to realize that where they were offered much more employment opportunity than the more developed countries. With the visitors' promise of housing, all the food you could eat, healthcare, unlimited training and entertainment coming true as long as you were employed, they reasoned that their location was preferable.

The biggest sticking point of the year was religion. With a world population so brainwashed by a lifetime of organized religion, it was understandable that people, while for the most part believing the broadcast statements made by the aliens, still held on to their lifelong habits. As it turned out, it was only when people started to turn up to their local churches on Sunday mornings to find them closed and shuttered by order of the government, that they real-ized they would have to accept the word of the aliens, or practice their faith on their own or in small groups. For some, this didn't sit well. For others, especially the charlatans, the loss of income and followers was devastating until they realized that there was no income, and they went on to find other ways to cheat people.

The atheists rejoiced, for they were, after so many centuries of opposition, finally vindicated. But even their adherents, after the reality finally set in, realized that humanity had lost a large part of its history, washed down the river of time, and a measure of its conscience.

The Roman Catholic Church, the Anglican Church, the Lutheran Church, the Baptists, the Mormons, Hindus, Muslims,

Islamists, and all other organized religions protested and petitioned the aliens to retract their statement, but to no avail.

Small splinter groups of religious fanatics formed and organized themselves into havens of enlightenment. Or so they thought, forgetting that the visitors could track them anywhere they went. As long as they caused no trouble, it seemed that the visitors had no reason to interfere with the small groups who refused to believe the proclamation. There was even one group that formed in what they thought was secret, who declared that the aliens were the gods come back to Earth.

For such a world-changing event, things went surprisingly smoothly. Of course, there were a few incidents, including a dictator who declared that his followers would declare war on the rest of the world if they went along with such a crazy scheme. Since he was widely known for his human rights violations and the abuse of power resulting in genocide within his own country, nobody was surprised when he disappeared, transported to one of the infamous holding cells aboard one of the visitors' prison ship. He would either be rehabilitated, or he would spend the rest of his miserable life there, unable to stir up more trouble. Leaderless, his followers soon dissipated amongst the people of that country.

PART 2

As the middle of the year rolled around, an emergency meeting was called, and as the assemblage gathered once again in the United Nations building, they knew all feared the worst, since this was the first time that Charlie had called for a meeting before the year was up.

The problems only seemed to escalate when fifteen minutes after the announced time, he had still not appeared. People turned to their neighbor or to their assistants to speculate upon the delay.

Time stretched, slower and slower, until it seemed everyone was looking at their watch every minute or two. An hour passed agonizingly slow.

Then, Charlie appeared with a bang. "Good morning. And I do apologize for the time you've been kept waiting. Unfortunately, we have before us a crisis, one not of your making, but it does very much concern the wellbeing of this planet. It seems that there has been an objection at higher levels to our attempt to bring Earth into the Continuum of Planets. There is one planet that is not satisfied with our level of progress in one area of assimilation."

All the heads of state were shocked at the use of the word *assimilation*, as many of them could still remember the reruns from last century of the TV program *Star Trek*, and the Borg, who attempted to assimilate humans with cyborg parts.

"Let me try to explain this problem to you. If you become members of the Continuum, you are going to meet and have to deal with many different species of sentient beings, some of which will be totally different to you. There are the Degarie, who are fifteen-feet tall and look like pale, skinny bears covered in a layer of fur. Then there are the Vuries, who live in a water world, with no land above water. They are covered in bright scales and can breathe both air and water. For visitors, they do have floating cities, but these structures do not float on the water. They float in the air, for their race has perfected anti-gravity. My personal best friend is a Ghando, who looks similar to an Earthlike praying mantis, except he has hands with five fingers instead of pincers. His name, translated for you, is Joe. There is also a race of sentient beings, all of whom look very much like your cockroach, except they are five feet long."

Charlie paused and slowly looked around the room to make eye contact with every person.

"The problem one of these planets has is that despite all humans being basically the same, there is still rampant discrimination based solely upon the color of one's skin. This, to them, is unacceptable, and it is a problem that we will be addressing in the next year. The main reason for the early assembling of this council was to prepare you for what is to come. It will probably take the rest of our allotted time here on Earth for a resolution of this issue to be made, as it is one of the most inexplicable and unacceptable problems within the human psyche, and we will have to eradicate it. It has been a mystery to us even though we have lived among you for a long time. This problem has been brought up early in this year so you would have the opportunity to return to your constituents to let them know what was coming down the pike.

"Unfortunately, this is an issue about which there can be no compromise. Therefore, it is up to the leaders of each country to educate all your people to insure that there is no discrimination of any kind at the end of the ten years. There will be no vote taken today, as this is a non-debatable issue. We will meet here again next January, when we will lay out our plan to solve this issue."

Amos sat stunned. He had been watching one of his programs which featured some skinny white guy who pretended that he was challenging the wild. It was, admittedly, one of his favorite comedy shows, and he watched it whenever he could, when he wasn't doing something more important, like cleaning his fingernails or picking his nose. The interruption was sudden, without prior warning and cut the skinny guy off in mid sentence. Amos sat and wondered what life would be like if the aliens were really able to carry this off. He had obviously served with black men before, even some that he had a fond affection for and one he was proud to call a friend, even though he hadn't seen him in years. But it seemed that there was a problem only with the one particular planet that Charlie had mentioned. Perhaps if the population of that planet were all black, that might explain the problem right there.

Amos sat back into the soft cushion which should have provided some comfort, but today was hard as a rock. He didn't know the solution to the problem, but to be truthful, he hadn't even spent much time thinking about it. But he was smart enough to know it *was* a problem; apparently a bigger problem for the aliens than it was for humans, which was a problem in itself.

Once again he found himself dozing off while contemplating the problem, but caught himself early enough to stumble into bed, his mind spinning with alternate possibilities.

PART 3

It was with heavy hearts that all the heads of state returned home to their countries, each of them pondering the impossible task set before them. Exactly how was one to change the minds of those who had grown up with discrimination as the norm in the places they had lived and with people who felt the same way? Also, how do you temper the resentment of those who had been discriminated against their whole lives?

A herculean task, but each of these leaders knew that they had to find a way.

As soon as Sylvia Han-Chin returned to the White House, she called a meeting of all her top advisors, in the Oval Office, searching for someone, anyone who might have an idea about how to handle this situation. Although many options were discussed, all the suggestions presented had a snowball's chance in hell of working.

Ben Williamson stood slowly from his chair of prominence in the center of the room, and fixed his gaze upon his boss, behind her desk.

"Madam President, I humbly suggest that through congress and the senate, sometime in the next few years, and certainly before the deadline, we enact an emergency amendment to the Constitution of the United States that states in clear language, that all citizens of the U.S. shall be required to sign a binding non-discrimination pledge, and those who do not, shall be executed. It is the only way we can save the planet."

Everyone in the room stopped halted. You could hear the walls breathe.

"You cannot be serious." Sylvia glared at him. "Such an amendment would tear the country apart. There would be nothing left to salvage from the race wars which would result from such a constitutional amendment."

"Sylvia, relax. Please, believe me, I was only testing your resolve. I am well-aware of the problem we face. After only a little over two years, the visitors have the population eating out of their hand, with their free power, free cars, free food, and free houses. And all the populace has to do is to keep working. It's sickening, the lengths they will go to earn the people's trust, when all they really want to do is to enslave us all."

"Ben, please go and sit down before you embarrass yourself any further. We are going to take a week to brainstorm this situation. I want you all to go back to your departments and agencies, talk with all of your people and come up with a solution to this problem. Call in anyone you need. And that is an executive order. Now, go!"

Amos was walking back to his cabin when he saw something rarely seen in the wild—a white-tail deer giving birth. He sat on a rocky outcrop and watched the progress of nature, and marveled at this miracle happening in front of him. Then he slipped away so as not to disturb the new mother and baby, and found a new way back to his cabin.

As he approached, he felt a tingling up his spine, something he had not felt since his last mission in Columbia. Amos slid to the ground. His view of the cabin was partly obscured by the red, orange, and yellow leaves, which gave the structure an ethereal quality.

All was quiet and still, the slight breeze rustling the leaves, but the feeling persisted. Nothing he could point to disturbed the idyllic setting, but something buzzing around in his head was ever present. He moved closer, noting the position of everything in his yard as it had been that morning when he set out, and found nothing out of place.

The closer he got to the back of the house, the more signals his brain registered. He then heard the low rumble of his TV turned way down, and relaxed knowing that a threat wouldn't be watching a TV program. Which could only mean one thing. Randy had finally found his cabin.

Amos stood and walked into his house through the unlocked back door. Randy sat in the easy chair facing the flat screen TV, watching a program about the mating habits of marsupials in Australia, drinking one of Amos's beers, and had already consumed three bags of Cheetos.

"Randy." Amos crept up behind the chair.

"Hey, Amos."

Amos had saved his life in Iran by pulling off a shot of over a thousand yards in the middle of a sandstorm, and Randy had been dedicated and loyal to Amos ever since.

"I didn't think you knew where my cabin was," Amos whispered.

A sly smile formed on Randy's face. "As a former Ranger, it wasn't that hard to figure out. I know you and your preferences, and I know how many miles you have on your truck each time you come to town to have it serviced. It had to be this valley or the next one over. And I know, for reasons which should be obvious, that you like to hold the high ground. You are so predictable."

"Well, next time you decide to drop by, call first," Amos said, a huge grin on his face.

"I would, except you don't have a phone."

"Oh, yeah. I'll have to get one of those, I guess." Amos sat on the floor, between the chair and the TV. "So other than raiding my kitchen, was there anything else that prompted your visit?"

Randy feigned indignity. "Of course there was. Sylvia called and asked for you."

"Why?"

"Hey, don't ask me. She didn't give me any details. Just told me to find you and get you to call her at this number." He handed Amos a slip of paper and a satellite phone. "It's encrypted." Randy stood, grabbed his beer off the table, and walked out the door to the front porch to give Amos privacy.

Amos dialed the number on the paper, and the other end answered on the first ring.

"Hello, Sylvia." He closed his eyes and could see her as she had appeared to him so many years ago.

The crimson pantsuit and the white silk blouse she always wore made her stand out from the rest of the crowd, and her long black hair assembled on top of her head in a severe bun, gave her slight stature the extra height she seemed to treasure.

"Hello, Amos. Long time." Her voice, as always when she wanted something, was pure honey, dripping through the ether with sweetness and viscosity.

"Yes, indeed. Why now?"

He was cautious because he had heard that cloying tone of voice a few times before, and the last time it had cost him everything except his life.

"I have a job that's to be right up your alley."

"Again I ask, why now? It's been almost thirty years. How do you know I haven't gone blind by now?"

She laughed quietly. "People have been keeping track of you, on my orders. I have made sure that you have been paid on a regular basis for your last job, so I just need you to do this last thing for me."

"Before money becomes extinct, you mean."

Even in the woods out the back of beyond, the news handed down by the aliens had made it.

She seemed startled that he knew, but recovered quickly. "Yes, there is that. But this job is vital for the survival of mankind and the planet."

"Not to put any pressure on me, right, Sylvia?" In his mind, Amos could see the smirk on her face.

"Now would I do that to you, Amos? You *are* my favorite assassin, you know."

"All right, enough flattery, you smooth talker. What do you need me to do?"

"Find a way to eliminate Charlie."

"That's a pretty tall order from what I've heard."

"Yes, but it needs doing." She could sense his hesitation, even from a thousand miles away.

"Why? Doesn't it stand to reason that he would have a second-in-command to help with controlling a thousand flying saucers all around the world. And besides that, he has told the world that he's invulnerable. Doesn't that kind of eliminate assassination?"

"Yes, it would. But we only have his word for that. Could be that he's lying."

"So you want me to go into the UN Building, find a firing position without anyone spotting me, and shoot him when he appears to speak. Have I got that right?"

"You will have help, and certain people will look the other way if they do spot you."

"And that's the other thing. Like everybody else, I have been following him in the news, and so far everything he has promised has come true. Why would you want to stop that?"

This was the sticking point she had debated with Ben Williamson on many occasions in the past couple years, with the same standoff occurring every time.

"Don't forget," Sylvia replied, "he has also promised to eliminate us if human nature doesn't change, and frankly I don't think all the people of the Earth have a snowball's chance in hell of changing enough to satisfy him."

"So at the next meeting," Amos said, "demand some guidelines, a goal to achieve, even a percentage to shoot for. Eliminating him, if that is even achievable, will not solve the problem. The real problem is that we *do* have a society which is exactly how he describes us. Our attempts should be focused toward changing the human psyche, as he said. Anyway, that's my two-cents worth."

Sylvia sighed. "While I agree with what you're saying, I don't believe it's achievable. We have to do something."

"Look, we both know what I am, but I don't believe I'm the solution in this case. While the greater part of the world agreed with my killing of the last man I eliminated, in this case I believe they would disagree."

Sylvia admitted defeat. "I suppose we could wait a while to see how things work out. After all, we still have seven years before our ultimate situation will come to pass. Perhaps we can come up with some way to measure the mood of the various countries of the world." She sighed, knowing that Amos's assessment was sound.

He let out the breath he hadn't realized he'd been holding, and felt his heartbeat start to slow from a gallop.

"At least for now," he said, "I think that it would make more sense to wait. With all the new things people will have to get used to, maybe the psyche will also be one of them. At least, I hope so."

"Yes. I do, too." Hope filled Sylvia's heart and mind, but she was not optimistic.

They said their goodbyes, with Sylvia making him promise to keep the phone charged and with him at all times.

Randy stayed the night and left early the next morning, minus the phone and its charger.

YEAR 4

PART 1

Nobody could have predicted what the world would look like when the time once more rolled around to Charlie's scheduled yearly meeting.

In some quarters, progress was being made at a crawling pace to settle some of the differences which had festered over many centuries in many parts of the world. Surprisingly, in some parts of America, long-held prejudices were being talked about, and in some cases, dealt with.

In the UN hall of assembly, having passed through the throngs of people gathered on the sidewalks and parks surrounding the building, the leaders took their seats. It seemed that the people, and not their government, had decided that this should be a national holiday.

The meeting started normally, with everyone anticipating the arrival of Charlie. He did not disappoint, materializing behind the lectern, where he removed his helmet and placed it before him.

"Greetings to one and all," he called. "I am so glad to see that you could all make it." He looked over the gathered leaders. "By now, some of the eagle eyed among you will have noticed the absence of King Faroud. In his place, allow me to introduce Bobby Umbotu, the leader of the country's opposition party, who has been appointed to be the nominal leader of what was the country of the Republic of the Congo until formal elections can be held. Unfortu-nately, King Faroud had taken the unprecedented step of using his troops to seize control of the supplies of food, water, and medical supplies we delivered to help the people of his country, and stored it in his palace. He apparently decided that the people should not have unfettered access to what they needed, without his control. He had even killed two people for trying to get needed supplies for their families. His plan to trickle down these vital supplies to his constituents, and his murder of these innocents, did not meet with our approval. Therefore, he and his top three generals have been placed in the aforementioned prison ship, in four cells from which there is no escape. They will remain there until the end of the allotted ten years, before their fate is determined by the newly elected government."

Charlie glanced around him, listening to a voice nobody else could hear, frowning at the news he was receiving. And then he disappeared from view, leaving his black helmet on the lectern.

The late January morning was crisp and cool, barely above freezing. At least it was bright and sunny, not like the week before, with a series of rainy days. To a mountain man, it was as close to Eden as a day could get.

Amos, intending to go into town for more supplies and to try to gauge the mood of the townspeople as to the latest proclamations from the aliens, was just exiting his cabin, and was walking up the well-worn path, headed for the beat-up old Dodge, when a tall man dressed in black appeared in front of him.

"Hello, Amos. Do you know me?" the man said.

"Y-yes, I do. You're Charlie."

"You are correct. We need to talk. Can you think of any reason why I might want to speak to you and you alone?" Charlie raised his eyebrows and tilted his head.

Thinking back to an earlier conversation, comprehension set in with sudden insight, and Amos found himself smiling.

"I can only assume it has something to do with my recent conversation with Sylvia."

"Again, you are correct. In her zeal to be rid of me, she has forgotten one important thing. Might you be able to tell me what that may be?" Charlie raised his eyebrows again, smiling.

"I'm afraid not, but I'm sure you are going to tell me."

"Oh, come now. You know that I'm talking about her minder. She has reported to me the entire conversation Sylvia had with you, but only from Sylvia's side of the phone. What I need to get from you is your side of that conversation."

Amos laughed. "Which I am sure you realize that you're not going to get."

"I understand your loyalty to Sylvia, since you've been friends a long time, but I have to tell you that whatever you said to her had a calming effect on her. I would only like to know what you said because I really appreciate that you said prevented me from sending her to the prison ship. As long as she sticks to what she told you, she will be able to carry on the duties of her position as president of the United States. At least until she comes up for reelection. I understand she is eligible for another four years."

Amos thought long and hard, running through the various scenarios and the consequences of his answer, before deciding that nothing could be gained or lost by answering truthfully.

"All right. I basically told her that she had nothing to gain by an attempted assassination, and that you were invulnerable, so any attempt would fail. You *are* invulnerable, aren't you? I also pointed out that everything you've promised so far has come to pass, so the better option was to wait and see."

Charlie nodded. "That is very perceptive of you. But to answer your question...yes, I am invulnerable. In fact, I could walk through a nuclear explosion unharmed. If you need more proof other than my word, would you like to shoot me with your sniper rifle and see for yourself?"

Amos was shocked. Not many people knew that he was a sniper, and certainly not Charlie.

Amos nodded. "I could do that if you wanted me to be certain."

"Go ahead. I'll wait right here."

Amos backtracked into the cabin, crossed the room to the fireplace, removed the piece he felt most comfortable with, and emerged with a .30-30 Winchester he used for hunting.

"Where should I aim for the most effect?"

"Anywhere you like. The result will be the same.".

Amos brought the rifle to his shoulder, aimed and fired. The rifle kicked as the bullet left the barrel. It hit Charlie right between the eyes...and bounced off and went singing into the deep woods.

To Amos's amazement, Charlie still stood before him, smiling, with not a mark on him, no blood, and he hadn't moved a muscle.

"So now you can tell Sylvia that her ill-conceived plan would not have achieved anything other than to put her into the prison ship." He paused for a few moments for Amos to gather himself. "I really must be going. The UN has waited long enough."

Amos was still shaking his head as Charlie faded from sight.

Once more, Charlie appeared behind the lectern at the UN, in front of a roomful of shouting people, each of them attempting to make themselves heard above the crowd. He waited until everyone had noticed his presence, stopped their conversations, and returned to their seats.

"First, let me give you my sincerest apologies for this brief interruption in the proceedings. It turned out to be something unavoidable."

Everyone held their breath.

Charlie paused to allow someone to ask the pertinent question, but for a long while it appeared that no one would go out on a limb to satisfy their curiosity. He was about to start again when a yellow light appeared from the POTUS.

He smiled. "President Han-Chin, you have a question?"

Sylvia drew herself up to the greatest height she could—beehive hairdo, platform shoes and all.

"Why have you asked us here for this meeting, only to disappear in the middle of it, wasting everyone's time?"

"There was a delicate problem requiring my immediate attention, and I'm afraid it concerns you, personally." He stared her in the eyes until she blinked from the intensity.

"W-what exactly do you mean by that remark?"

"During this brief period I've been away, I have had the opportunity to meet with your would-be assassin, and I found him to be enlightening." Charlie beamed as she stood dumbfounded.

"What!"

"Yes, Sylvia...if I may call you that. I went to have an enlightening chat with one Amos Richardson at his cabin in the backwoods, where he shot me with a .30-30 Winchester."

"Honestly, I don't know what you are talking about!"

"Really? I would have thought it was obvious."

She bristled with indignation. "I am not going to stand here and be insulted by you, making these wild accusations without any proof whatsoever." She moved to leave.

"You can, of course, leave if you wish. However, your seat will have to be taken by someone who will represent the United States in your place. The people who reside in your country should have some kind of representation in the affairs of the Earth." Charlie was shaking his head, strangely reminding Sylvia of her father, years ago, when he was disappointed with her. "Your minder has reported your side of the conversation with Amos. In fact, she has even recorded it. Would you like me to play it back to you to remind you of your conspiracy?" He crossed his arms.

"I...I didn't know...that I had a *minder*."

"Sylvia, first I would like to remind you and everyone here that you all have a minder. Second, you have no idea how close you have come to joining King Faroud and his cohorts on the prison ship. But since you are one of the few of these leaders that I like, and even admire, I have made an exception in your case, provided you can assure me that nothing like this ill-advised conspiracy of yours will ever happen again."

She stood frozen. "I suppose that, after all these years, Amos is not as good as he used to be, and he missed the shot?"

"No. He is still as good as he used to be. He actually shot me right between the eyes. The bullet bounced off me because, as I've indicated on several occasions, I am invulnerable to all Earth weapons, as are all my men, women, and ships." Charlie looked around, daring anyone to contradict him.

Sylvia glared at him. "All right, Charlie, you want assurances that I won't attempt any further actions against you or your conquering hordes, and since I seem to be powerless to do anything about it, I can give you that assurance. But as leader of one of the most powerful nations on Earth, I demand that you give us some kind of assurances as to our future. Some kind of goal which we can attempt to strive for. A percentage to aim for to keep from being incinerated."

Charlie laughed. "Madam President, this is not high school. You don't have the luxury of a passing percentage, an A, B, C, D or F. This is an all-in-or-bust scenario. A live-or-die situation which you cannot change. If you and the rest of your so-called leaders of the world cannot convince all your people, in the next few years, that our way is better than yours, and to comply with the wishes of the Continuum of Planets, then your planet is doomed."

She bristled. "And those, sir, are the words we would expect to hear from a dictator!"

"After all we have done for the people of Earth, I cannot believe what I am hearing, madam. Do you seriously expect me to believe that you think your citizens are not better off than they were before we arrived? Given all we have accomplished in the short time we have worked together, don't you believe that the world is better off than it was?"

Sylvia smiled, and with that honey-dripped voice, replied, "But of course we are. Anyone with half a mind can see that. But consider at what cost? In our history, we have already had a great number of dictators, kings, and multi-billionaires who thought the world should run to their timetable and perception. And they were wrong. That is precisely why the people who actually care about their country and the world, like me, kept assassins like Amos around just in case there was no other way to deal with the situation. While I admit that it's an extreme measure to take, it should indicate exactly how I feel about this situation that we, the people of the Earth, are facing now. We did not ask you to come, and what you are proposing is an invasion of not only our territory, but also of our minds. Naturally, you could send dissidents like me, and many others who think like me, straight to your prison ship, but since this broadcast is livestreaming to the people, the world would know what you have done."

Hovering over her desk, Sylvia leaned over and banged her fist onto the button to light up her red light.

Boris stood and did the same. It took only a few moments for all the other heads of state to catch on, and soon the whole board was glowing red.

PART 2

For the first time in a long while, Charlie was annoyed. He also seemed to be at a loss for words, and stood silently, scanning all the heads of state who had rejected him.

"Without a doubt," he said, "I don't understand what you are thinking. I have heard that most men on this planet do not understand what their women are thinking, and I find myself in that uncomfortable situation right now. Could you please explain yourself. What exactly is your problem?"

Sylvia replied, "If you have lived amongst us for as long as you claim, you surely must realize that humans, people of my planet, do *not* enjoy being told what they *have* to do. We are a people of free will, and ultimately *have* to have a choice, and the decisions must be ours alone to make. You and your storm troopers leave us no choice. It's your way or the highway. And while ours may not be a perfect system, every person has the right to stand up and say no!"

"Assuming I can get my superiors to agree," Charlie said, "what exactly is it that you want to happen?"

"You are demanding of us an all-or-nothing solution to a problem that has existed since man evolved into a thinking human being. It just isn't going to happen. There will always be people who think differently from the majority, and they should be allowed to do so as long as they do no harm to anyone else. You are demanding a robot population in which everyone thinks and acts the same, and it is just not going to happen. As long as the people of the Earth exist, there will always be those who think and act differently. It is just human nature."

Charlie thought for a long time.

"Sylvia, while I can understand what you're telling me, you and all the people of this world will have to look at it from my perspective, too. We, the people of the Continuum, whom I represent, are concerned that your flawed way of thinking will have a detrimental effect on the peace we now enjoy due entirely to the rigid rules in place across the universe, to which everyone adheres. While we do appreciate your predicament, we have come here in an attempt to make you see the light. The eleven billion people here on this planet are but a mere drop in the bucket compared to the hundreds of trillions of sentient beings in the Continuum."

Sylvia sat and rested her head on her folded arms on the table.

Boris replied, "I, too, am of the opinion that the task you have set us is unachievable, considering the upheaval that is a constant in our world. You seem to be like our old King Canute, who set his throne at the low water tidal mark and commanded the tide not to wet his feet as he sat upon his throne. It didn't happen then, and it is not going to happen now. That's all I have to say."

Sylvia finally raised her head and stood. She looked around the entire room, noting that most of the leaders were nodding at her.

She finally looked Charlie in the eye. "Charlie, I have a proposition for you to take back to your superiors. Upon the approval of all the world leaders, I propose that, in the next six years, we will attempt to educate those who are willing to change, identify those who are not willing, create new worldwide laws to stop all the discrimination, and imprison those who break these laws. I don't know how many people each group will include, but if your superiors are willing to accept our supreme efforts to eradicate the problem, we, as a people, will do our best."

Charlie was slow to respond. "While I personally would accept your proposal, I do have to take this back to my superiors for approval. The meeting is over. I will inform you of our next gathering. Thank you all."

Charlie disappeared.

PART 3

Amos leaned back in his favorite easy chair, in front of the TV, and smiled as the UN meeting came to an end and the talking heads started to analyze what everyone already knew.

That's the Sylvia I knew way back when. He tuned out the pundits' psychobabble.

Despite that she'd been married for thirty-five years, Amos had loved her for all that time, but never had the nerve to tell her.

He knew that what lay ahead of the human race was not going to be solved by an assassin such as him, but by a steady, all-encompassing program of education, persuasion, and even coercion. Those with the most to lose, as always, would be the hardest to convince. But the alternative was something Amos didn't care to think about.

It was weird that his life-long profession was now unnecessary. Maybe he ought to be thinking about getting some free training in a new field.

If he was honest with himself, though, he had gotten fond of this initially-forced but eventually-chosen lifestyle. He had always been a loner, and enjoyed his solitude, isolated in his backwoods cabin, and slumbering in the quiet embrace of Mother Nature. His biggest regret was the loss of so much pristine wilderness, and the man-made pollution which had created it.

Amos thought long and hard about what he was destined to do with the rest of his life, and could not come up with any viable solutions. He supposed he could become a forest ranger—he at least had the training and expertise for that. But then again, he would be accountable whoever was one step up the ladder from him. Try as he might, he could not see himself in that role.

Of immediate concern was where to get his supplies. He knew Randy would continue to supply him with the necessities, but he was worried that Randy might get into trouble with the aliens' proclamation for helping to maintain the lifestyle of what Amos was, an undocumented shirker living off the hard work of others, and it bothered him. Not so much the shirker part, but for the problems he might cause for Randy.

Sometime after midnight, Amos fell asleep in the easy chair in front of the TV, which was still filled with dire predictions from the talking heads.

I'll deal with it tomorrow.

YEAR 5

PART 1

According to those who witnessed the event, the incident started off harmless. On the evening following the latest United Nations broadcast, the most talked about subject was the visitors' incredible announcements, and what could be done to comply with their demands.

A black young lady was seated with her boyfriend at a dive bar in Queens, New York, where she took another slug of her third tall whiskey.

"Well, I for one, think that this is a stupid idea," she blared. "How can they expect us to put aside many generations of thinking in just a short six years? Personally, I have no problems with white boys, black, Asian or even Hispanics. It's the women I have a problem with."

Her raucous laughter echoed through the hubbub of the bar, and a few people stared at her.

"And that's exactly the kind of thinking that is going to get the whole planet incinerated in a few short years," said a voice from the far end of the bar.

Everyone turned toward the speaker, and the young lady pushed herself up from her high-top barstool, wobbly, and struggled to see him over the heads of the crowd between them.

"What the hell do you mean by that?" she said.

The speaker, a tall white man in his mid-twenties, also stood. "Well, I for one, can see that the plan that they have laid out for us has a snowball's chance in hell of working as long as prejudiced minds such as yours cannot accept that we have no choice in the matter."

"All my life I've been told what to do and where to go by white men, the woman said, "all of them making threats against me. And as far as I am concerned, this guy Charlie is just another one of a long line of them. I am not going to change the thinking I've been brought up with just because another honky threatens me. Besides that, I am certain God will look after us and show us the way to defeat him. Anyway, where is he going to hide from God if he blows up the whole world?"

Her antagonist shook his head and smiled. "I am willing to bet that just as many black men as white have told you where to go and what to do, but you chose to rail against the white man because of your upbringing. Believe you me, I understand where you are coming from because I was brought up in the deep south and taught from an early age to hate black people. But as I grew up and moved about the country, even before the coming of the aliens, I changed my way of thinking, and I now hold the view that all people are just that—people. We all have our faults, but if we all respect one another, there is no need for discrimination, especially due to the color of your skin, which nobody has any choice about. And God? I'm sorry, but don't expect any help on that front. Were you not watching when Charlie told you that he and the others like him were the ones we revere as our gods? After what I've seen, his actions could have been considered miracles by the unsophisticated people who lived back then. What I don't understand is that seemingly educated and enlightened people today still cannot see their way past this fairy tale that is organized religion." He shook his head once again, then sat and took a long pull at his beer.

The woman's boyfriend, a tall, muscular black man, listened to his girlfriend's whispered remarks before he stood stalked toward the white man seated at the back.

"You can't talk to us like that, putting down our beliefs just because you don't want to believe."

"I am not putting you down. I just don't understand."

"Perhaps if you paid more attention to the word of God, you would not have these feelings of antagonism against black people." The boyfriend moved closer to the white man, his fists clenching and unclenching.

The white man backed toward the rear wall as the crowd parted for the black man, who was quickly closing the distance between them. Then a figure dressed all in black appeared out of thin air between them.

"Stop!" The figure outstretched his hand, and the boyfriend halted.

The figure had no accent, but his speech was stilted, as if English was not his first language.

"You will leave the premises now, and I would advise you to contemplate what Charlie has revealed to you. There is no God, and while I must admit that I did enjoy the adoration I received when I played the role of Saint Francis of Assisi, I want you to know that what I wrote was all fairy tales, conjured up in my own mind."

The black man clapped his hands over his ears and retreated back to his girlfriend.

"I don't want to hear it! You cannot disparage my beliefs. There is a God, and he will dispatch you demons back to the hell you came from as long as we believe in Him."

He grabbed his girlfriend's hand, and they stormed out of the bar.

The figure in black, an intervener, turned toward the white man. "You should be more careful about where and when you express your opinion, even if it is the right one."

He faded from sight, leaving behind palpable disbelief among the patrons of the bar.

Richard Adams was seated at his home office desk, and lowered his face into his tear-soaked hands, his leather-patched elbows planted on blotter on the desktop.

For more than an hour now, he had contemplated on the problem he faced, but still with no solution in sight. What seemed to be so easy for others to deal with seemed like an insurmountable obstacle to his way of thinking.

Richard had been an accountant for his whole working life. He was married and had two wonderful children, but his whole life revolved around numbers and the clients who brought them to him to fix. His spare five-foot-eight, one hundred-forty-pound frame and his alabaster white skin spoke volumes about his lack of exercise and outdoor activities. His hobbies were non-existent, apart from the occasional crossword puzzle, never having indulged in what he considered time-wasting pursuits. His greatest pride was having accumulated enough money to ensure his family would survive if he were to die.

Now, with the aliens' proclamation that there was to be no more money, his whole world had collapsed, and he had no idea of how to fix it. To him, it didn't matter that he and his family could have anything their hearts desired without costs. Richard had no idea what to do with the rest of his life. At forty-nine years of age, he felt too old to retrain and had no desire to do so.

He was not one given to histrionics. The few friends he had felt Richard had no emotions at all, and they would have been shocked to see him in his present state. He had spent the past hour sobbing and feeling sorry for himself.

He was startled to feel a hand upon his shoulder. He raised his head and turned to find his wife, Colleen, staring down at him.

"Are you all right?" she said.

"I don't know. I don't understand what's happening to me." Richard shook his head and wiped at his tears with his sleeve.

"Come to bed. It's after midnight. Things will look better in the morning." She bent down and wrapped an arm around his shoulders, and attempted to make him stand.

"I sincerely doubt it." He rose unsteadily to his feet and wrapped his arm around her neck, then kissed her cheek.

Together, they drifted toward the bedroom and undressed and slipped into their night clothes, facing away from each other, as had become their ritual for the past ten years. In the past few years, their sex life had gone from intense passion to daily routine to grudging obligation to non-existent. Colleen turned the lights off, and they slipped into bed, keeping their distance.

"Good night," she said.

"See you in the morning." Richard tried to sound cheerful, but it obviously didn't work, for there was no response from the other side of the bed.

Again he felt the prickling at the corners of his eyes as once more the tears threatened to come. He closed his eyes and tried to think positive thoughts.

It didn't work.

After four hours of random thoughts and no sleep, Richard raised his head from the tear-soaked pillow, slipped from under the sheets, and padded to the bedroom door. He opened it, thankful that he had finally lubricated the squeaky hinge that Colleen had been complaining about for the past six months. The kids were no problem, for they had slept through a category 2 hurricane down in Florida. And besides, their bedrooms were on the other side of the house.

Richard tiptoed to the kitchen, and ignoring the bottle of Famous Grouse Scotch sitting on the counter, he opened the fridge. After ten minutes of contemplation, he emerged with a bottle of water, and carried into the office.

He stood in the middle of the room for a good five minutes, then moved to his desk and placed the water on the desk, with a coaster underneath. For a few minutes, he tried to remember why he had gone down there, but then remembered and went to the wall safe, punched in the combination on the electronic keyboard, and opened it. This was where he used to keep all his ready cash, important papers, and the thing he now sought, his gun. The gray zippered case was still in pristine condition, and smooth to the touch. He removed it from the safe and laid it on the table.

Richard sat in his swiveling desk chair and removed the gun from its case. It was a snub-nosed .38 Special he had acquired in his youth, when he had imagined that a man who dealt in finances would sooner or later need to defend himself. It had only been fired five times, the total bullets in the revolver. It had then been reloaded and filed away in the safe, never to be seen again…until now.

He released the cylinder, spun it once, and dropped the five bullets into his hand. They felt heavy.

Richard closed his eyes, trying to rationalize what he was contemplating, but discovered that he could not justify his drastic course of action. He wondered what gun oil would taste like, and considered leaving a note on his computer to the manufacturers of gun oil to put Tabasco sauce in with the oil to make it unpalatable to those contemplating suicide.

As he sat there, facing east, staring through the half-closed blinds, in the predawn hour when all was blackest and coldest, he had a revelation of sorts. Some might have called it an epiphany, but since he was not religious, he preferred to call it a sudden glimpse of common sense.

He realized that the five bullets he was rolling around in his hand were at least twenty years old, and the chances of them firing were low.

Richard leaned back in his chair, chuckled, then rose and returned the gun and bullets to the safe. He went to the kitchen, poured himself two fingers of Grouse, and threw in a couple rocks, then headed out onto the covered deck. He sat in an old recliner which had seen better days, and balanced his drink on the arm of the chair.

Despite the early morning chill, he was beaming when the sun finally peeked over the horizon, and the Grouse helped his focus as he contemplated his future with hope and enthusiasm. His family was going to survive, even if it was only for the next five years, according to the aliens' timetable.

Relaxed by the alcohol, Richard fell asleep on that old recliner and slept soundly.

PART 2

Smiling to himself at the sight before him, Charlie was seated at his favorite place on the ship. Here in his sealed ready room just off the main bridge, which had been outfitted with the most well-engineered and exquisitely upholstered commander's seat in the entire fleet, he felt more at home than in any other place.

As Charlie would be the first to admit, he did like to indulge in his creature comforts. Not coincidentally, his *throne* also happened to be situated in front of the most comprehensive surveillance console on the ship. Charlie insisted on keeping a weather eye on all things at all times, for he was not one to be caught napping. On this console, he could call up live video of any location, not only on his own ship, but on all the ships in the fleet, and any location on the planet Earth by means of microscopic cameras. He could also review recorded video and audio from those same places.

Charlie was currently watching a feed from a bar in Queens, New York, where a young white man was trying to convince an equally young black woman that her attitude was what was going to get the planet incinerated. The strident woman's boyfriend seemed to be listening to the white man's arguments, at times even nodding in assent, but the woman clearly was not, and she was making sure that her boyfriend was on board with her point of view.

Charlie sent a short message to his aide to provide an intervener, a guard who would place himself between opposing parties, for the young white man.

He was puzzled by the double-knock upon his door, for his entire crew knew that you did not disturb the old man in his ready room unless it was for something only he could handle.

After shutting down the screen, but keeping the feed alive, Charlie disengaged the security locks on his door.

"Come in."

He was surprised when the head of his ship's medical unit inched in.

"Commander, would now be a good time to discuss something which I consider of extreme importance?" the doctor said.

"But of course, Doctor. Please come in and make yourself comfortable."

"Thank you." The doctor moved over to the closest guest chair to the consol.

"What can I do to help you with this matter?"

"I have a situation for which I have no explanation or recourse, and I need your input."

"Explain."

"Our men are falling ill and dying."

"What! From what?"

"I don't know, and that's my dilemma."

"What are the symptoms?"

The doctor hesitated and tore his gaze away from his commander.

"The disease seems at first like a mild nasal infection, which is why I put out a fleetwide announcement for all persons suffering nasal congestion to report to me personally. You may even have seen it on your own com screen."

Charlie vaguely remembered the note and thinking that the doctor was trying to scare up business for his clinic, simply to keep from getting bored to death.

"I remember seeing it, but at the time I thought we were all immune from something as simple as a sinus infection."

"We are. But that is not what this is, unfortunately."

"So what is it?"

"I don't know. I have checked all the databases of all the planets, and even old medical texts from Earth, and nothing even comes close to an explanation."

"How many?"

The doctor closed his eyes and whispered, "Over fifteen hundred are sick so far, and one hundred dead. And it has been only three weeks since the first case appeared."

"Good grief. What are the stages a patient goes through?"

The doctor consulted his notes. "Stage one, the patient complains of a sinus infection, which turns out not to be mucus, but cerebrospinal fluid from the brain invading the sinus cavities through weakened membranes. Stage two, the patient is overcome with lethargy and only wants to get more and more sleep. Can't eat or drink, can't keep anything down. Stage three, they are sleeping for twenty-four hours, and eventually lapse into a coma. They are usually dead twenty to thirty hours after that. But the strangest thing about this disease occurred when I did the autopsy on the first death. When I made the first incision, his body dissolved and ran down the drain of the autopsy table, in a reddish-brown liquid. The only thing left was the brain chip implant. Even the skeletal structure and organs had dissolved. I decided to allow two days to elapse before I attempted an autopsy on the second man to die. What I found surprised even me. Apparently, time has an effect on this decomposition, for when I made my initial incision on the second man, no liquid flowed. While all the internal organs and skeleton had been dissolved, the intact skin had kept the fluids contained, and they eventually congealed into a Jell-O-like consistency."

Charlie sat with wide eyes. "Could this be a weapon against us?"

"I very much doubt it. How would they get it onto the ship?"

"Have the victims been placed in quarantine?"

"Of course. It was the first thing I did. And only a few of my staff know about the problem. Each of the doctors on the other ships have been told to transport their patients exhibiting the symptoms directly to the sick bay on this ship, and so far they have all complied with that order. Hopefully we can keep it contained to those already infected."

"I want the name, rank, and serial number of every patient, and any who come after them. I want to find out where they've been and who they've seen."

"I can already help you out there. Every one of them has been down to the planet recently, all of them as seekers, but some doing double duty as minders."

"Are there any cognizant enough to answer questions?"

"Most of them are until they enter the latter stages. Keeping them awake is the problem. They all realize that there is something seriously wrong with them."

"Then let us go and talk to these people and see what we can find out."

"You will have to take precautions. You must wear a full bio-hazard shield at all times."

"That's not a problem. And doctor, I want to thank you for bringing this to my attention. I'll make sure that it is mentioned in dispatches next time we communicate with our superiors. Maybe a promotion or a commendation will be in order."

"Thank you, Commander. But I didn't do this for promotion or recognition. I did it to save our people's lives, nothing more."

"Of course you did. Excuse me for the misunderstanding."

They left Charlie's ready room together, the doctor who leading the way. Charlie wondered what the confrontation in the bar in Queens had come to, but then put it out of his mind.

When they arrived at the medical center some twenty-five minutes later, Charlie was surprised to find himself out of breath, possibly due to the blistering pace the doctor had been moving at. *Or maybe it's because I've been doing a lot more transporting than walking lately.*

"While I realize that you do not have as much free time as I do, Commander, you might want to think about getting some exercise into your daily routine. Some of the hiking trails up in those mountains, besides being beautiful, can be exhilarating and are great for your cardiovascular system. They are also a quiet place for contemplation."

As they entered the small facility, identified only by a tiny bronze plaque next to the door, Charlie was struck by the silence. The doctor led him down an overly bright, white corridor to the double doors at the end of the passage. As they approached, the doors swung open to admit them to an open floor plan ward with multiple beds screened from one another by free-standing, movable walls. The doctor then led Charlie to a bed five in from the door, and turned right. The patient raised his eyes without any expectation in them, but widened when he saw Charlie. He struggled to raise himself out of bed to stand at attention, until restrained by the doctor.

"No need for ceremony now," said the doctor. "We are just here to ask you some questions. Commander..."

"What ship are you from, son?" Charlie said.

"Fleet four-zero-two, sir."

"And what is your specific duty?"

"Up until I got sick, I was the minder for the prime minister of Canada, sir."

"In the two weeks prior to your illness, did anything out of the ordinary happen that stands out in your memory?"

The patient hesitated. "Yes, sir. I was invited by the prime minister to attend a barbeque with his family and friends, and to disguise myself as a guest in order to mingle with the other people. I requested and received the necessary permissions from my commander for this. Keeping in mind my seeker role, I also had intimate relations with a young woman."

"Why does this stand out in your mind?"

"I know there were strict orders against it, but after one year of dried rations during the transit from our home to here, I just couldn't resist the temptation."

"Resist what?"

"I had my first taste of human meat, and it was delicious."

"You what?"

Charlie could not believe his ears. That order took precedent over all others.

The look on Charlie's face must have told the patient he was in deep shit.

"But, sir, the prime minister insisted that I join them. Told me it wasn't often that he could sit down with family and friends to enjoy this meat which they called venison. Apparently, it's rare."

Charlie released a breath he didn't realize he'd been holding. He stood still for a long while, and then walked drifted to the window to gaze over the long verdant vale to the mountains beyond, the ones the doctor had mentioned on their way to the clinic. The beautiful interiors of all of the ships, despite their stark outward appearance, were reproductions of villages on their home world. Large tracts of woods and open fields were interspersed with roads and streams, and several ten-thousand-foot mountains dominated the center of each ship, allowing the population to indulge in hiking and mountaineering, and on some ships, skiing. There were even small bars and restaurants in the countryside and villages.

Finally, while still facing the window, Charlie said, "I cannot pretend to be pleased that my most important directive was so easily broken, and there is still no positive proof that the consumption of this *venison* is the cause of the illness. However, there is nothing I can do to you as punishment that you haven't already done to yourself. Doctor, I will count on you and your colleagues to question as many of your patients as are cognizant about their imbibing of human meat, and then report back to me. Have you determined yet whether this disease is infectious or not?"

"It appears as if it is not, at least in the last three weeks. All the patients I have seen so far have been down on the planet at some point, and those they have been in contact with since they have returned are not showing any signs of the illness."

"Then I'll leave you to your work. Use as many resources as necessary, but bring me some results."

Charlie turned and strode from the building. He waited until he was hidden by a hillock before calling for the transporter beam to take him back to the corridor in front of his ready room. He used his remote to let himself in, thinking about this unusual problem at hand.

Jerry awoke.

At least, he thought he did.

He opened his eyes.

Or at least, he thought he did.

All was blackness. Not even a glimmer of light grazed his wide-open eyes, even though he strained to discern his surroundings. The air was heavy, oppressive, weighing him down, pinning him to the hard, cold surface he lay upon. Even breathing was difficult.

He tried to move his left hand up, but it seemed glued to the surface. He was no more successful with his other hand, despite the strain he exerted.

The hold extended to his head, for although he could move it from side to side, he could not lift it from the surface. His legs and the rest of his body could also be moved from one side to the other, but not up.

He felt as if a great force was pushing him down, allowing him only a slight movement, but squashing his body to the smooth surface below him.

From his attempts to manipulate the extremities of his body, he discerned that he was naked. This was not a great worry to him, as he often slept without clothing, except in the coldest conditions.

"Hello?" he called.

Even his own voice seemed deadened and far away. All else was disturbingly quiet. Not a breath of wind, or the normal sounds which seem ever-present, disturbed the dead silence in which he found himself.

Or did he?

Was this real? Or was it just a vivid dream?

In the past, Jerry Sanders had found himself in unusual situations. Once, he found himself in the middle of the day, choking on the heat and sand of the desert in Iraq. But strangely, the phenomenon happened while he was enjoying a ski vacation in the Alps.

His skiing buddies, and the psychoanalyst to whom he later related this event, all told him that he was nuts and it was all in his head. Jerry wrote it off as one of those unexplainable things, and forgot about it.

Now it came back to him in flashes in the darkness, and he shuddered.

Were they right? Was it all in his head? Was he going crazy?

Or was it real?

When it came, the intensity of the bright light overwhelmed his optic nerves, and he raised his hands to shield his eyes. With that movement, he realized that his body had been released and was free from the constraints he had been fighting all night.

It took a while, but slowly Jerry was able to open his eyes and observe his surroundings. He was inside a cube, and noted that there were no windows and no door. His furnishings consisted of the bed he was lying on, a built-in platform on the floor, with rounded corners and a hard pad imbedded into the composite material which everything in the room seemed to be made of, a combination commode and washbasin, and a desk with a built-in chair. Everything was a brilliant white.

Jerry stood, and in a few seconds had walked the entire room. The temperature, humidity, and quality of the air had changed from oppressive to pleasant.

He jumped at the a plate materializing on the table in front of him. Upon this gift were three rashers of bacon, scrambled eggs and hash browns, two pieces of buttered toast, raspberry jam, along with a glass of apple juice and a cup of black coffee. Everything he would have prepared for himself under normal conditions. There was even a stainless steel knife and fork, and a cloth napkin. Jerry realized that he was ravenous, and set to eating with a vengeance. Everything was hot and delicious.

He had barely finished eating when the mess before him disappeared, right down to the smudge of jam he had dropped on the table, and the ring the coffee cup had left.

"Who are you, and what do you want with me?" he said to the blank walls.

No answer.

He sat there for what he thought to be over an hour, alone with his thoughts. He was had no idea of the reason for his incarceration. Jerry did suspect, though, based on his recollections of Charlie's speeches, that he was being held on the aliens' prison ship. As far as he could recollect, he had committed no crime.

A thought formed in his mind, but he brushed away. They could not possibly know about that incident, since it had been hidden away under the table by the authorities. Still, the memory kept nagging at him, and the details came to mind.

When the black and blue burger appeared on the table, Jerry concluded that it was lunchtime, and once again they had chosen one of his favorites. He was glad to see that they were not going to starve him to death. He was concerned, though, about the whole morning of total silence he had endured. He enjoyed having stimulating conversations with people of his own intellect, and the enduring silence was already starting to get on his nerves.

Lunch finished, he was once again left alone with his thoughts. He used the commode, an advanced design which used no paper or water, but left him feeling purged and clean. He washed his hands in the sink, but instead of sitting at the desk, as he had during the morning, he walked the few steps over to the bed and lay down.

He closed his eyes, but the brightness of the room prevented him from falling asleep. He supposed that this situation was by design. A prisoner could not dwell on his mistakes if he were in dreamland.

Even though he racked his brain for the whole afternoon, he could not remember any transgressions that were serious enough to land him in this torture chamber, except for that one, and surely he had made up for that mistake.

The afternoon passed slowly, and since Jerry had no sun upon which to judge the passage of time, he got up from the bed and wandered in circles around the diminutive space in an effort to get a little exercise. He was making his one hundred and tenth circle, when he was surprised to see another of his favorites appear on the table. A rack of lamb with mint sauce, and a salad with blue cheese dressing was done to perfection, and they had even included a glass of his favorite beer.

He ate slowly, savoring each mouthful, and knowing full well that at the end of this sojourn, they would once again subject him to that unnerving darkness he had awoken to that morning.

Sure enough, as the last morsel of the meal was consumed, the plates and utensils disappeared, and surprisingly they allowed him to use the commode, before extinguishing the lights.

With little choice, Jerry lay on the bed, and the sensation of being held down reasserted itself. The air thickened, and the feeling of being trapped came back with a vengeance. Thankfully, with three good meals and an afternoon of exercise behind him, he fell asleep quickly.

The next day was a repeat of the first, but with differing details. Blueberry pancakes and pork sausages with orange juice for breakfast. Two tacos for lunch, and a slice of Beef Wellington with vegetables and a beer for dinner. And then the long night under the restraints of the aliens' control. Jerry thought that this might be the scenario for the rest of his life. Or at least, until he found out the allegations against him.

On his third day of captivity, just after breakfast, he was wondering if he was to spend another boring day introspecting himself for flaws, when the white wall before him became filled with words—

Do you remember June 15, 2017?

Are they really going to drag that up again?

Please answer. We can hear you, the wall instructed.

"Yes, I remember."

Please explain.

He thought back with a growing unease.

"I was a green ROTC sergeant in the Afghan War, but I was placed in charge of a platoon of soldiers, and we were supposed to infiltrate a village in the Hindu Kush. One of the men behind me tripped and accidentally fired off a shot. All the doors in the village opened and people started rushing out into the street. With no other choice, we started shooting. And before long, there was no return fire. Dawn was breaking, and we had time to reconnoiter the village, but we found only the bodies of fifteen children and two adults, all from the orphanage in the town. We realized the mistake we had made, so we then concocted a story about being attacked by enemy combatants, therefore having to defend ourselves. Despite all the indications against it, the Army accepted our version of what happened, and shortly afterwards they sent us home."

After the initial accidental shot, who fired first?

After a long pause, Jerry replied, "I did."

And your men followed your lead?

"Yes."

Can you think of any reason why you should not be charged with seventeen counts of murder?

"No." He hung his head in shame, tears prickling at his eyes, threatening to overflow.

There was a good five minutes of hesitation, before the next words appeared on the wall.

You will be returned to your home tomorrow. But a file of your transgressions will be forwarded to the JAG Corp for further consideration.

"If it makes any difference, I am truly sorry for my actions that night. I was inexperienced, and I have spent the last thirty-five years of my life working with and helping orphans whenever I can."

Yes, that has been duly noted and will be included in the report that we submit.

Jerry spent the rest of the day regretting having told the Army a different version of what happened, but was convinced that there had been no malice behind his actions. It had been an accident of war, similar to friendly fire. He only hoped the Army saw it the same way and would allow him to continue the work he was now doing with his children, for he had come to see them that way.

His last two meals aboard the aliens' ship were less memorable than the first ones, and he went to sleep that night under the same oppressive conditions he had now accepted as normal.

He awoke the next morning in his own bed, in his own home, ready to accept the verdict of the JAG Corp, and ready to continue his crusade if they would allow him to go on with it.

PART 3

If Jason Stein had stopped to think about what he was about to attempt, he probably would have given the whole thing a miss. He had already seen the footage of the explanation from Charlie that all the visitors were impervious to any form of physical harm, including any human-developed weapon.

At twenty-two, Jason was being impetuous, a common trait shared by many of his fellow scientists at MIT. He was much younger than most of them, only fourteen when he was hailed as being a child prodigy. Besides, he was sure all that malarkey where the aliens claimed they were able to make themselves invisible was probably just a bunch of misdirection on their part to frighten people into submission.

Jason's specialty was industrial and military-grade lasers, and the application of these designs. He had developed a theory that if he could concentrate a laser beam on one of the visitors for a sufficient amount of time, they would boil away inside their shells. It seemed logical, and it should work, given the laws of physics.

Through the magic of advanced digital printing, he had already designed, manufactured, and built a weapon using his theoretical concept of long-term laser exposure. The weapon he carried, the LTLE-1, was the same size as a 9mm Glock pistol and was much lighter due to its high-tensile plastic construction. He was anxious to test out his theory, and had convinced himself that, should his theory prove wrong, he was prepared to lay down his life in the attempt. He reasoned that, although he couldn't recall any of the aliens carrying weapons, an attack on one of them was sure to bring some kind of retaliation. Though, the attacks on their ships had brought no reaction from them.

The biggest problem Jason had was finding a subject to test his experiment upon. Although he had wandered the streets of Cambridge for over a week now, he hadn't found any aliens, for he had seen no one dressed in all black. The only alien he had seen was Charlie, and that had been on TV.

Frustrated once again in his search, and noting that it was getting close to dinnertime, Jason decided to suspend his wandering and return to his dorm. Muttering obscenities, he turned in a circle before ambling toward the university. As he descended the hill, he was startled to feel a presence behind him, and jerked around to came face to face with a materializing dark figure only a yard away. The man was smiling at him, his face aglow with amusement at Jason's bewilderment.

"Jason, good afternoon to you," the man said.

"Wh-who…who are you? Where did you come from? Wait, are you Charlie?"

"No, Jason, I'm not Charlie. Although, others do say we look alike. You can call me Fred. I am your minder." The man still had a broad smile plastered on his face.

"What do you mean, my minder?"

"I have been assigned to keep an eye on you."

Thoughts of espionage ran through Jason's mind. "To what end?"

"Charlie was concerned about that little popgun you've invented, and asked me to ensure that you don't hurt yourself or others with it trying to strike at one of us." The man's smile faded.

"So my theory was correct? This is something that can hurt you?" Jason pulled the LTLE-1 from its holster and held it barrel down in both hands, watching the man's reaction.

He was unnerved when none came.

The man's smile came back to its full intensity. "No, it is still incapable of hurting us in any way, but we are concerned that you or someone else may get hurt or even killed by it, especially since it is so unstable."

"What do you mean, unstable?"

"Since you are one of those scientists who merit special attention, I have been with you the whole time, invisible and in the background. I was there behind you when you did the final calculations for the strength and resilience of the plastic for the gun, and saw when you subtracted instead of added the reflected heat from the time frame of the laser. The effect is cumulative, so if you fire the laser more than twice, it will disintegrate, taking your life with it."

"I don't think I believe you. I would not have made such a simple mistake. I think you are afraid that I am going to use this gun on you."

Jason raised the gun to Fred's chest, less than a foot from the man.

Fred was still smiling as he made no attempt to move away or defend himself.

"So pull the trigger and let's get the doubt out of the way. I promise you no harm will come to either of us."

"I don't know. Are you sure?"

"Well, don't you want to kill us all so you can take back your planet? Do it!"

Jason's pulled the trigger, and a brilliant blue Argon laser beam jumped to Fred. The man smiled through the five seconds it took for the gun's power supply to exhaust itself and shut down. As promised, neither man was hurt, the energy having been absorbed by Fred's shield.

"And so you see, Jason, it did nothing detrimental to me. You have one more shot out of that weapon before it blows you to kingdom come, if you want to risk it. My advice is to take it home, disassemble it, and destroy it before someone gets hurt. Recalculate your parameters and recreate it from a fresh perspective. It is a viable weapon and effective, except on us. My only question to you is, why do you need it? With no more money, no more territorial disputes, and no more armies, why build a new weapon? I cannot understand why you fight amongst yourselves, especially now. You all have the same benefits—a beautiful healthy planet, all of the food, drink, recreation, travel, enjoyment, and opportunity you could want—and still you insist on making things difficult for each other. Can you please tell me why?"

Jason hung his head in shame. "I don't know. I truly don't know. Perhaps it is because that man has always had to fight to get what he and his family needed to survive, and it has been so ingrained into our psyche that we know no other way. I don't envy Charlie in his task of trying to change the everyone on Earth's mind about how to survive, because that's a task that will take generations, not merely years."

Fred finally stopped smiling, and his face grew dark. "Unfortunately, I fear you are right. But we don't have generations, only a few years, and unless someone comes up with a solution, your planet will not survive the purge that is coming."

Jason walked a few feet over to a park bench and plopped down. He placed his elbows on his knees and lowered his face into his hands, weeping. Fred followed to sit beside him and place an arm across his shoulders. Not a word was spoken for a long time, the atmosphere full of sorrow, and darkness crept upon them as they sought a solution to a seemingly insurmountable dilemma.

After an hour, Jason regretted that his shortsightedness had overcome his sense of right and wrong.

YEAR 6

PART 1

No one was surprised when the sun rose on another glorious sum-mer's day. Just as nobody had been surprised five years ago at the hurricanes, tornados, and droughts all over the world, the melting icepacks on the north and south poles releasing millions of tons of greenhouse gasses into the atmosphere, exacerbating the problems already caused by the burning of fossil fuels to expand humans' excesses in comfort.

All of that had changed with the arrival of the aliens, who within the first year had brought such dramatic changes to the Earth's environment that people, even cynics, had to admit that the course they had followed for so many years was flawed. Many were stunned by how quickly the Earth had repaired itself when allowed to do so, and billions of people benefited from the aliens' intervention.

With the aliens' intercedence of Earth's traditional social conventions, millions of starving people were saved, and the elimination of borders allowed the world population to become participants in a plan to allow everyone to get their fair share of available resources.

The only people at risk in this scenario were those rich, money-grubbing millionaires and billionaires who preyed on the common man, never allowing hard-working men and women who furnished the source of their excessive personal wealth, an even chance to get ahead because of their nefarious schemes to strip the little guy of everything he had.

A surprising number of suicides occurred due to the elimination of money, because many of the moneymen discovered that they had no skills to offer in this strange new world. Now you were judged on what you could offer the general populace, and not on how much money you had.

With bated breath, the world waited for the the annual State of the World Address, conjecturing on what new challenges the aliens could bring to the table, for everyone expected something marvelous.

The State of the World Address was to once again be held at the UN Building, but this year, with a conciliatory nod to the leaders of the world and their constituents, Charlie, instead of materializing behind the podium, chose to walk into the building, showing everyone that he did not consider himself above them.

He did not claim the head of the procession, either, stepping aside for Sylvia, the POTUS, Queen Gretel of Sweden, the Prime Minister of Australia, Heather Hawkins, and the Premier of the Polish Republic, Velma Kruschenko. He also deferred to Boris of Russia, and walked into the hall, arm in arm, with the King of England, Charles, who had recently suffered the loss of his mother, Queen Elizabeth II. Everyone could not help but notice that, although Charlie was going out of his way to be gallant, there seemed to be sadness in his demeanor.

All in all, it had been a strange year, mainly due to the unlikely alliances formed around the world. To everyone's surprise, North and South Korea got together, and over a period of several months, formed a union which seemed to be working. Taiwan and Mongolia rejoined China, and the Balkan States signed a nonaggression and trade pact which equally favored all.

Iraq, Iran, Syria, Lebanon, Jordan, Egypt, and Saudi Arabia sat with Israel at the bargaining table, and in ten months, came out with a package designed to keep them all from each other's throats, at least for the foreseeable future.

The Caribbean Islands, having been in competition with each other for a long time, especially for the tourist dollar, formed the United Islands Federation and promised each other an equal share of the influx of tourists, since everyone could go to the Caribbean for free.

PART 2

Charlie strode to the podium and remained silent to allow the assembly to finish their conversations. When the room had finally quieted, he placed his clasped hands on the lectern and smiled.

"Welcome once again to this annual meeting. After a great deal of consideration, we have decided, since we have eliminated all national borders and boundaries, that we will, with your permission, have to rename this assembly." He could see the question mark in everyone's eyes.

"From now on, it will be known as the One World Council, and it will be responsible for overseeing the affairs of the planet. This will ensure that one part of the planet does not receive preferential treatment over another." He scanned the room.

"My friends…I hope I am allowed to call you my friends, because I have done everything in my power to encourage that feeling in you and in myself. If there is anything you can think of that disqualifies me from that designation, don't hesitate to let me know what you feel I have done wrong." Again he scanned the room, and found no dissenters.

"What I have to report to you here today hurts me to my core. Some of my men, those who, for one reason or another, have visited Earth and then returned to their ships, are dying of a mysterious illness. So far we have no idea what is causing it, and therefore have no way of combating it. We have conducted a thorough search through our own archives, as well as all of the Earth's databases, but have turned up nothing that can help us find a cure. It does not appear to be infectious since it is confined to people who have visited the surface of the Earth, and any others who have been in contact with them seem to be in perfect health."

His normally placid face seemed to crumble as his account of the symptoms and final consequences of the illness brought an almost unanimous wave of sympathy from the crowd. Only a few muttered, "They got what they deserved."

"I am not sure if any of the pre-eminent doctors of Earth are able to help, but we would be more than grateful if they tried."

"So why are you still around?" a heckler shouted, from the lower ranks. "I mean, you claim to have been here for hundreds of years, and I am sure you have made many trips to and from your ship, but you do not appear to be sick or dying to me."

"I am not," Charlie replied. "But I do not have an answer for you as to why."

Sylvia and Boris both stood.

"We have many highly qualified doctors in the U.S." Sylvia said, "as I am sure Boris has in Russia. We would be more than happy to attempt to find out what has happened to your people."

"I second that," Boris said, "The doctors in Russia will be standing by to help in any way."

PART 3

It was late afternoon when Charlie finally launched his diatribe.

"Hatred is an abomination. So is envy and lying and cheating. Anyone who hates someone else because of the color of their skin, the slant of their eyes, their lifestyle, their wealth or privilege, is exactly the person we wish to eliminate. While we have terminated a lot of envy with the elimination of money, much envy is still caused by someone else's inherent beauty, intelligence, athleticism, or raw talent. While we cannot excise the cause of all envy, we can and will work to exacerbate it. While I am aiming these comments mainly at the United States, Europe, Russia, and China, to this day the caste system still remains in India, China, Japan, the Philippines, and Indonesia, as well as the tribal prejudices in Africa. I could go on, without even mentioning the Middle East, but I'm sure you get the general idea."

Boris Chevsonenko struggled to his feet and leaned his bulk against the table to remain upright.

"Charlie, excuse me for interrupting you, but I am just trying to clarify a few points you made earlier."

"Of course, Boris. Please go ahead."

"Given the ten-year deadline that you established six years ago, do you seriously think mankind can change multiple generations of hatred and prejudices in just a short three years?"

A stricken look flashed across Charlie's face. "I don't know if it's possible, but that is the deadline I've been given by the overseers of my expedition here to Earth, and I will comply with it."

"Personally, I don't care about your deadline. I'm here to tell you that it is impossible. Mankind is not going to change that rapidly regardless of whatever threat has been presented. It's just not going to happen." With a wheeze, Boris regained his seat, the effort exhausting him.

Sylvia stood. "Much as it goes against the grain, in this case I have to agree with Boris. Three years is not enough time to negate the animosity and prejudices that have grown, handed down from parent to child, over multiple generations. You are asking a leopard to change his spots. And while I would like to see it happen, I don't think it ever will. At least, not in the time frame which you have set." She turned around to gauge how many people agreed with her assessment, and found countless nodding heads.

For first time in his dealings with humans, Charlie was speechless, not only from the refusal to cooperate, but because the majority of heads of state had finally agreed on something without a vote being taken.

Charlie shook his head in frustration and disbelief. Did they not realize that it was only a choice between ridding themselves of the ill feelings toward their fellow human beings, or being annihilated? After all, feelings that had once been learned as young children could be unlearned by thinking adults, and eventually forgotten.

Charlie closed his eyes for a few moments, and with considerable effort, tamped down his frustration. When he was finally under control again, he delivered what he hoped was an inspirational message of hope.

"Actually, I am pleased with the progress that has been made so far. My scouts, working in conjunction with the minders, have reported that vast areas of the world are now starting to cooperate with each other. They are actually looking out for their neighbors, cooperating, and forming alliances, where not more than a year ago, they were fighting. It's remarkable, really. And while many amongst you may feel that the task that has been set before you is impossible, we are encouraged by what we see. Now all that remains is that good people double their efforts to bring the die-hard fanatics around to the way things ought to be."

Tommy Hernandez boat was being docked on the Miami River. He was proud to finally be able to call himself a commercial fisherman.

For many years, the industry had seen a steady decline in productivity and profits. Due to the pollution of the world's oceans, the decrease in the amount of fish that could be pulled from the water, combined with the ever-increasing limits permitted by the world's governments, had produced a toxic atmosphere between buyer and seller when it came to making a decent—hell, even a meager—living as a commercial fisherman. Strangely enough, the many inventions which had been developed over the years to help the fishing industry catch more fish, and which had been outlawed due to lack of fish, were now starting to be allowed back again due to the increase in many species because of a healthier Earth.

These days, though, Tommy was smiling a lot. With his new boat, powered by one of the alien power cells, and without a lien on it due to there being no money in the world, he felt like he was in hog heaven. Mind you, it was still hard and dangerous work, but it was what he had been doing all his life, and he didn't want to change it for the world.

Ever since the cleanup of the world's atmosphere a short six years ago, the most notable effects had transferred to the oceans, resulting in ever-increasing stocks of fish available, which caused the governments of the maritime nations of the world to declare that the limits were to be removed from many of the species of fish for which he hunted. Where before he had usually returned to his base of operations with only a half-load of questionable fish, he now came back with his boat loaded to the gills with only the finest fish of the catch, the rest having been released to live for another day.

Tommy had another reason to be happy. Since there was no more money, there was no reason to haggle with the buyers of his bounty. After keeping a few of the best fish for himself his family, and his crew, he turned the rest of the catch over to the distributors without animosity. He was no longer required to work his usual seven days a week since he could easily catch the government's full-time fisherman quota in two days, and could therefore spend a lot more time with his family and friends. And that was worth a lot more than the now non-existent money.

He even noticed that the normally cantankerous fishermen on many of the other boats now helped and cooperated with one another since there was no need for competition. Some had even become friends, or at least drinking buddies, something which would have been unbelievable only a few years ago.

For Tommy, life was good.

YEAR 7

PART 1

Josh reached the top step of a townhouse in Georgetown and rang the doorbell, but nobody answered. Unusual, since he had been summoned to this house by his superior officer. Well, at least, by his former commander when they were both in uniform.

That had been over five years ago, and Josh had not thought about Colonel Harrison Miller in the intervening time. Not that he held any animosity toward the colonel. They'd had a number of satisfactory missions together, and had been honorably discharged on the same day during the drawdown after the aliens' appearance, and had parted as friends, promising to stay in touch. But the difference in status between an officer and a non-com meant that, despite good intentions, it had never happened.

When the summons had arrived on the colonel's crisp white embossed stationery, Josh's wondered, *How did he find me.* Josh had been around the block a few times since his discharge, moving from place to place without reason and without plans. He had no permanent home, and no friends or family, so he simply drifted.

Before the elimination of money, his government pension had allowed him to be wherever he felt.

He had been staying at an inexpensive hotel in El Paso, Texas, when the manager had brought him a small brown paper package addressed to Sgt. Josh Jackson, Room 103, Grand Hotel, and told him that it had been hand delivered by a soldier. By the time Josh had opened the package, the soldier was long gone. Inside, he found the colonel's instructions to appear in Georgetown at this specific date and time, and $10,000 cash for expenses. Why the man had had sent it was beyond comprehension since money did not exist anymore. All Josh had to do was book himself on a flight across the country.

His bewilderment was interrupted by footsteps behind him, and he turned to face the colonel.

With smile on his face, the Colonel said, "Sergeant Jackson."

"Colonel." Josh almost saluted, but caught himself.

The colonel mounted the steps, and grasped Josh's hand. "It's good to see you again, my boy. Come inside."

"Good to see you, too, sir."

"You can drop the *sir.* I'm just Harry to you, now."

"Yes, sir—I mean, Harry."

Harry smiled and turned the doorknob to lead them inside. He hung Josh's coat on the rack and walked him into the library. He offered a drink and a cigar, both of which Josh declined, and then sat in an easy chair by the fireplace, then indicated the second chair to Josh.

"Josh, you're probably wondering why you're here." Harry leaned back into the chair.

"The thought had crossed my mind, Harry."

"It has been a few years now since I've had the benefit of your council, but now I find it necessary to once again count upon your unique way of thinking."

"I'm afraid I don't understand what you mean."

"Really? I'll let you in on a little secret, just in case you didn't realize it." Harry sat up straight. "For the last few years of our service together, I had come to rely on your assessment of the situation, and act accordingly. That is the only reason I rose in rank faster than anyone else. Including you. I stole your ideas, tactics, and plans, and presented them as my own. And for that, I am sorry."

"Harry, you didn't steal anything from me. I gave you what I thought was the best solution, and since I knew nobody else but you would listen to what a non-com from Alabama had to say, I freely gave you information, knowing you would see them implemented."

An awkward silence hung heavy, neither man knowing how to break it.

Finally, Harry rose and walked over to the bar, dropped two ice cubes each into two glasses, and filled them with three fingers of Knob Creek. He gave one to Josh and sat back down and took a large swallow.

"Now I find myself in a situation where I need your help again. I need your insight into how to deal with the aliens at the end of this ten-year ultimatum they have presented us with, if they do indeed intend to exterminate us if they are not satisfied with our progress. What do you think?"

"Who do you work for, Harry?"

"What makes you think I work."

"Don't bullshit me, Harry. You wouldn't have flown me all this way, or for that matter, gotten hold of actual currency, unless you are connected to some agency."

"I never could fool you, could I? You're right. The president asked me to form a think tank to come up with a solution for getting out of this dilemma. I thought of you immediately, but it has taken months to track you down. Valuable time which could have been used more productively."

"But why would you choose me?"

"Because I have never met a more clearheaded, outside-of-the-box thinker than you. Someone who always comes up with a workable solution to any problem."

"You do realize that flattery won't get you anywhere, don't you, Harry?"

"Then how about I give you a challenge? Sylvia asked me for the best, and that's what I'm going to give her."

Once again, suffocating silence filled the room. Josh took an occasional small sip from his glass. Time passed, and the ice in their drinks melted. Harry, even after all the years apart, was already used to the almost trance-like state Josh went into when he was tackling a problem.

The first three days passed in frustration. Try as they might, they could not think of a solution to the insurmountable problem of certain people's unshakable hatred of other people.

The best that Josh could come up with was a worldwide media blitz sending the message of peace and love to as many people as possible, while explaining what would happen if the aliens were not satisfied. They sent their conclusions to Sylvia, who read them with disdain, but authorized their implementation.

After several weeks of negotiations, almost all of the world's heads of state composed and sent to the One World Council management, an audio and video file of their speeches stressing peace, love, compassion, acceptance, and concern for the future of the planet. As someone said, when asked about the aliens' promised destruction of the Earth, *If the collective minds of mankind remained unchanged, there was no Planet B.*

Shortly thereafter, these speeches pushed most commercial messages off the airwaves, and even political messages suffered from inadequate exposure.

It took a while, but it appeared that friction between adversaries seemed to be diminishing, proving once again that even an unpopular message, repeated often enough, could become accepted as truth.

Most people hoped the efforts would be enough to satisfy the aliens' agenda. But many feared it would not.

PART 2

Charlie once again walked into the Council Chambers, shook hands with many heads of state, and assumed his position behind the podium.

"Welcome to our seventh year together, and the second year of the One World Council, the organization and stamina of which has exceeded our expectations as to their influence and scope. In this session, I hope to encourage you to continue down the path you yourselves have chosen, and hopefully come to the conclusion that a better world awaits those who chose to put aside their lifelong prejudices and hatreds in favor of tolerance and acceptance of those different from themselves. The world is made up of all kinds of people, but they are all people of Earth and have the same rights and expectations as everyone else.

"On a more somber note, we have learned of a group of operatives who are debating the possibility of resistance to our plans, even up to the point of attempting to find a way of harming us. Now, as has been pointed out many times, and even demonstrated, we cannot be harmed by any earthly weapon. Not our people, or our ships.

"This group, while I am sure their intentions were honorable, nevertheless seemed to be plotting against us. We therefore sent a number of our invisible minders into their midst. What we found was that they were not plotting against us, but attempting to come up with a solution of the problem of human prejudices. And while we did not see a whole lot of progress in the time we spent with them, we wish to encourage them to keep trying anything they can come up with.

"One thing I am pleased to report is that the fatal illness that struck my people who returned to our ships from Earth appears to be dissipating. No new cases have been reported for several months now. But unfortunately, all fifteen hundred seventy four people who contracted the sickness have passed away. At this point, we do not believe it was a weapon of Earth aimed at us, but a naturally occurring event as yet unexplained. Unfortunately, we still have no idea what it was or how to cure it. And while we grieve for those lost, we are not contemplating any kind of retaliation."

A few days later, Charlie, in his ready room, keeping an eye on developments, received a tentative knock on his door.

Now what.

He walked to the door and opened it, and was surprised to see the doctor standing there with a smile, holding his cap. Charlie inclined his head and motioned him inside the room with.

"I have good news."

Charlie raised his eyebrows and walked behind his desk to sit.

"We have found the cause of the disease afflicting our men, and a cure for it!"

"Well, Doctor, don't keep me in the dark."

"How much do you know about molecular biology?"

"About as much as I know about quantum physics. Not much. Why?"

"Let me try to put this in layman's terms. All living beings have DNA, and most have chromosomes. Human beings on this planet have chromosomes, as do we. The human male has XY chromosomes, and the female has XX chromosomes. We have something similar. Our females have ZZ chromosomes while our males have XZ chromosomes. Are you with me so far?"

"Yes, I think so. You are basically saying that we and the human species are compatible genetically, right?"

"Wow, good analogy, Commander. Unfortunately, that is not quite right. If you think about it, you will recall the industrial accident that occurred on our planet two hundred or so years ago."

"What about it?"

"You remember that the accident affected all the males on our planet and has turned them impotent? The accident initiated our search of the universe for a compatible species that will allow us to carry on instead of eventually dying out."

"Yes, yes, I know. What about it?"

"We came across an abbreviated report, a short note in the archives from one of our earlier expeditions to this planet. Not an officially filed report, since it mentioned a problem with the compatibility of human females with males of our species, but did not mention any specifics, since it was not specifically investigated. After a series of experiments, we have ascertained that the damaged Z chromosomes of our males are reacting in a detrimental fashion with the X chromosome of the human female. In fact, it is deadly."

"Are you serious?"

"Yes. To put it simply, human females are killing our males. Mind you, not intentionally, but because of the damage to our Z chromosomes."

"Then we need to recall all male seekers back to their ships, regardless of their current status."

The doctor held up his hand. "Sir, I have already done that. I hope I haven't overstepped my authority, but I felt it was imperative to get them all back before we lost any more of them."

"Thank you, Doctor. You did the right thing. Do the female seekers have the same problem?"

"Apparently not, since we have already had many successful births from the ones we sent out when we first arrived, both male and female babies, and all seem to be healthy. We also have many successes from previous expeditions. If it was up to me, I would recruit as many female volunteers as possible to go down to the planet to get pregnant. The more volunteers we can get to participate, the better. Everyone we can recruit to enlarge the numbers, can only mean that our gene pool is as large and diverse as we can make it."

"Go for it."

The doctor hurried off.

There might yet be hope for our planet, as well as Earth.

PART 3

Peter Jensen glanced at his brand-new, gold Rolex Submariner and saw that the end of his five-hour shift at the Dunn Family grocery store was only three minutes away. As a stock boy for the chain of stores, the thought of him ever acquiring such an expensive watch would have been a stupid idea even a year ago. But since the aliens had outlawed money and put everyone on an equal footing, he had been lucky enough to snag one before they had all been snatched up. Of course, it had been a simple matter to make as many as there was a demand for, using the replicators, but his was an original, and not an alien-made duplicate.

He thought ruefully back to those days not so long ago when he had to work six ten-hour days, without benefits, just to survive, and silently thanked the aliens for their mandates, since there were now plenty of workers to fill the spots, which were five-hour, four-day work weeks, with six weeks of vacation each year. Everyone received full medical, dental, and vision, as well as their choice of sports, exercise, and recreational pursuits. This situation Peter was particularly thankful for since it left him with plenty of time to engage in his passion—old-fashioned film and digital photography.

He had already acquired, from alien sources, four-by-five, eight-by-ten, and thirty-five-millimeter camera equipment, darkroom enlargers, trays and chemicals for film processing, and printing, digital cameras, and computer programs necessary to carry out his unique visions.

Since every square inch of the earth's surface had already been photographed by Google Maps, travel photography was a saturated field, so his vision took him into unique, unexplored fields where only he could produce the photographs that people were beginning to appreciate and collect.

Single, shy, and withdrawn, at twenty-two Peter was most comfortable in his self-created reality without the necessity of either male or female companionship, or even pets. As soon as his shift was over, he walked the half-mile to his one-bedroom walk-up, and let himself into the self-decorated flat with a palm print. He made himself a large mug of Earl Grey tea, and carried it over to his computer chair. He wasn't a teetotaler, but he hadn't had a drop of alcohol in months, reasoning that he didn't need any outside stimulation to create his art.

Peter sat, and with a wave of his free hand, the chair conformed to his shape and lowered to the point where he felt weightless. The mug of tea even had its own place, and slipped in without spilling. Again, a palm print worked its magic, and the chair powered up, lowering the screens over his eyes and taking him to his latest creations. The controls for the computer were mounted on the arms of the chair, and he manipulated them with thought.

He was pleased to see that the two images he had placed on the Internet the night before had already been downloaded over ten thousand times each. He was also intrigued by an invitation from an art historian by the name of H. H. Banyon, asking him to meet at a place of his choosing for an interview to appear in Art World, an e-magazine he had a monthly subscription with. Since Peter was a homebody, he had to Google a restaurant to meet at before setting a time the following afternoon. The affirmative reply came back immediately.

The mundane necessities taken care of, he transitioned to his latest creation in progress and spent the next two hours in bliss, manipulating the subtleties of color and light in a fashion known only to him, since he had written the program he used on his photographs.

Once he finished for the day, he Googled H. H. Banyon to find out who he would be meeting the next day, but no match could be found. That was strange. Peter thought Google knew everybody. He then entered his own name and got a through description of his short life.

The five hours at work the next morning seemed endless, especially the seven-to-midday shift when all the complainers from the day before came in to voice their miserable opinions. But when it was finally over, Peter hurried home, determined to give a good accounting of himself. Why he cared, he wasn't sure, since there was nobody he wished to impress. Perhaps the possibility of a job offer somewhere other than the market was a primary motivation, but he didn't have any training in anything other than film and photography.

He was shaved and showered and dressed by three, for the half-hour walk to the restaurant where he would meet this stranger at four. He expected to be home for dinner.

Peter was seated early, allowing him to examine the surroundings. He was pleased at his choice, for the clientele was upscale, and he reasoned that if the place was bad, or even indifferent, they wouldn't be here.

Right at four, the front door opened to reveal the most stunning woman he had ever seen. She strode into the place with a cloud of confidence surrounding her. His breath was snatched from his body, and his heart pounded.

She spotted him and came over, holding out her hand. "Hello, Peter, I'm Helen Banyon.

He did not remember standing, but there he was, shaking her soft hand and gazing into her clear blue eyes, which regarded him with a hint of amusement.

"Hello," he heard himself say.

"May I join you?" she said, her voice soft.

He snapped out of his trance. "But of course. Please sit."

He held the chair out for her, and when she was seated, he sat as well.

"Please forgive my impropriety. I was not expecting a beautiful woman."

"Why, thank you, kind sir. Your compliment is much appreciated."

"Forgive me again, but why H. H. instead of Helen?"

"I've found that I get more interviews if I don't reveal that I am a woman until the interview." She pulled a digital recorder out of her purse. "I find that I am more accurate when I record the conversation. Is that all right?"

"Yes. Yes, of course. It's not as if I will say something to incriminate myself." He chuckled.

"So, shall we begin?"

"What would you like to know?"

"Anything about you or your work that I can't find on my computer would do just fine."

The interview lasted an hour and a half, and then they had a pleasant dinner together.

That night, a virgin Peter Jensen had his first sexual encounter. His last thought before falling asleep was, *Life is good.*

When Peter awoke the following morning, he was upset to find that the new love of his life had disappeared from the apartment. He searched everywhere, but couldn't find her. He knew she still had to be somewhere in the apartment because all the locks on the doors and windows were still locked.

Helen stood in the ready room with Charlie, watching the frantic search in Peter's apartment, which was doomed to failure. She felt sorry for Peter, but he was young, and would soon forget her as he encountered more females of his own species. She was certain that a man such as he would succeed.

"So, the doctor has confirmed your pregnancy?" Charlie said to his wife.

"Yes. Although, when he asked if I wanted to have a boy or a girl, I told him I just wanted a baby, and he smiled as if he knew which it was."

"Whatever the sex of the baby, we will raise him or her as our own. You have done well, my love."

YEAR 8

PART 1

Captain Alan Jamison, head of the Violent Crimes division of the Broward County, Florida, Police Department, was frustrated.

Well, perhaps not frustrated. Severely bored better described the way he felt. Working a six-hour, four-day shift was not something he had ever envisioned doing at the beginning of his career. However, with violent crime down 99 percent, his time was mainly spent filing paperwork of old cases, and researching cold cases, with the help of the aliens' video and computer systems.

The few new cases which found their way to his desk were filed with the aliens' vast computer database, and anywhere from a few minutes to a few hours, depending on the complexity of the case, an answer would come back to him with the perpetrator's name and current location, and Alan's job was simply to dispatch several officers, sometimes as many as fifteen, to pick him or her up. When the case went to court a few days later—since there was no more backlog to contend with—the preponderance of the evidence usually produced a guilty plea, and justice was served.

One of the few pleasures of Alan's position was assigning officers the plum jobs to cover the many musical and sporting events which were now held daily in various stadiums around the county. Due to the proliferation of free time that everyone enjoyed, the musical groups and other entertainment companies that had stayed together for the artistry and not the money, found themselves with a multitude of venues to play.

The sports scene also flourished. Athletes who played for the love of the game found many new places to compete in. The adoration of the fans was still the number one draw.

The least favorite part of Alan's job was assigning traffic cops, because of the tedium of the position. With traffic accidents down by 98 percent, due mainly to the sophisticated anti-collision systems built into the latest surface and air cars, and the proliferation of auto-drive systems, even drunks could get home safely, but there were still some old junkers out there driven by those who refused to move, on and who managed to collide with each other many times each year.

Getting on in age, Alan was looking forward to retirement, but every time he calculated his own personal timeline, it always came back with the same answer. He was due to retire a few weeks *after* the aliens destroyed Earth, for he believed that people would not change enough to satisfy the aliens' desires.

PART 2

Charlie was once again seated in the luxurious chair in his office on the capital ship, indulging in what had become his favorite sport—eavesdropping on certain members of the human race. He was currently tuned in to a lay preacher who was trying to convince a group of his followers that what the aliens had said about God was untrue, and showed that they were not to be trusted.

Charlie smiled. *I'll have to mention this fellow at the meeting next week. There must be something that can show him just how wrong he is.*

His thoughts were interrupted by a knock on his door. He frowned, remembering the last time someone knocked on his door, and the consequences that came from that.

"Come in. It's open."

The door was opened by the science officer, the man responsible for the fleet's computer database.

"I'm sorry to disturb you, sir, but I have a report to give you, and thought it would be better if I delivered it in person."

"Come in and sit down. Let's see what you have."

"Yes, sir."

The man sat stiffly in the center seat of three, facing Charlie, and seemed hesitant.

Finally, he said, "There seems to be a glitch in the computer system. People dropping off the DNA grid."

"What!"

The DNA grid allowed them to track all the people on Earth.

"I'm sorry, sir. Perhaps I should explain."

"Yes, perhaps you should."

"All the ships did a software upgrade last week, one that was sent from central command and was ordered installed. Since that upgrade, we have noticed, and the computers have confirmed, that between one and two billion people have been dropping off the grid for between one and six hours at a time."

"How is that possible? Is it the same people all the time?"

"No. Sometimes it is the same people, and sometimes not. But we have found out why it is happening."

"Why?"

"When a person drops off our grid, it is because they are wearing some kind of head covering. A motorcycle helmet, a baseball cap, even a yarmulke, or a sheet of tinfoil, for all I know. It is really perplexing, sir."

"And you know this, how?"

"We had a minder with a certain person when he dropped off the grid, and it occurred when he donned a baseball cap in order to go and play a game. He came back on the grid when he removed his cap. We have since then tried experiments with many head coverings, all with the same results."

"Who knows about this?"

"You and me, and the top science officer on each ship."

"Not central command?"

"No, sir, they have not been informed as of yet. That decision remains with you, sir."

"How serious do you think this is? What is your assessment?"

"It is probably not all that serious. As long as the subjects of the DNA grid don't know about it, they obviously are unlikely to exploit it."

"I agree. Would you be able to back the upgrade out of the system if it became necessary?"

The science officer looked sheepish. "No, sir. Unfortunately, the upgrade overwrote several million terabytes of data concerning the previous system's parameters, which weren't archived."

"OK. I'll inform central command. Keep this information confined to those who already know, and see if there is a way to override or correct the glitch."

"Yes, sir. That's why I came to you personally and did not inform you over the com system."

"You did the right thing. Go back and see what, if anything, you can do to fix the system."

"Yes, sir. And thank you, sir."

PART 3

"Once again, welcome to you all. This is our eighth year together, and the third year of the One World Council. I have encouraging news to impart to you, and a dramatic demonstration which should dispel all doubts as to our veracity."

Once again, Charlie stood before the heads of state, who sat with rapt attention.

"First, you should be encouraged by the news that I am sure you have all heard by now. A formal and binding agreement has finally been reached between the former state of Israel and the Palestinian people of the region, and for that I applaud the leaders and the people of both parties. My fervent hope is that the people concerned will now live up to the agreement and not just give it lip service. Having seen the results, that of a population changing their minds overnight on other planets, I feel encouraged that, here, too, we can all live together in peace and harmony. In disguise, and sometimes invisible, I have travelled throughout the region, and overwhelmingly, the outlook has been positive. The ordinary people are saying, loud and clear, thank God it is over." Charlie smirked.

For the first time in the eight years of these gatherings, another figure materialized behind him. A woman dressed in black, just like him, but with a figure to die for, removed her helmet and gave him a radiant smile before placing it on the lectern next to his. Her long, silken black hair reached to the middle of her back between her shoulder blades, and shook in rippling waves whenever she moved her head. With a pride born of a long, loving relationship, Charlie placed an arm around her shoulders and drew her close.

"Ladies and gentlemen, I would like to introduce you to my wife. This is Donna. She is my rock when I feel that I am slipping, my inspiration when I feel lost, and my companion when I feel unloved and unwanted. I would never have made it this far had it not been for her constant presence and encouragement."

The chamber erupted in thunderous applause, and her pale face turned rosy as she stepped up to the microphone. Her crystal-clear bell-like voice was in sharp contrast with Charlie's gravelly voice, and she could have sung harmony with Julie Andrews in her heyday.

In a faraway city, Peter Jensen sat up straight and his jaw dropped to the ground.

"Helen."

"Thank you for your warm welcome." Her sharp blue eyes made every man enthralled, and every woman jealous. "I have chosen to stay away from these proceedings until now since I felt that I had little to contribute, other than supporting my husband behind the scenes. I am here today to make a simple appeal to the women of your planet. I wish to ask your help in ridding this world of the fear, prejudices, and racism it has held on to for far too long. Help me educate the children of the Earth to be loving, fair, and not to discriminate against anyone. No child is born with fear, hatred, or prejudice in their hearts. They are taught that behavior, usually by those closest to them. We women have the power to control how our babies turn out. Let us endeavor to make our strongest attempt to ensure that they turn out to be the adults that we can be proud of in every way."

She glanced around wistfully at the crowded chamber, still smiling, but a cloud of sadness had crept into her features.

"Ladies, be respectful of your men, but not subservient. Your opinions, concerns, and feelings matter as much as theirs do. You have as much say in the upbringing of the child as them. And men, you need to be respectful to your women, whatever relationship they bear to you, because they deserve it, and without them there would be no more human race."

A deathly silence had fallen over the chamber as the stunned audience sat contemplating their own thoughts.

"I feel I may have gone too far in my enthusiasm, and for that I do apologize. I do, however, firmly believe that men *and* women are created equal, and should be treated that way. I also believe that both parents are responsible for bringing a child into this world, and therefore should have equal responsibilities for the upbringing of that child. And that child must be given the best care, comfort, and education two parents can bestow on their offspring.

"I will leave you now, to defer to my husband, who is so much better at this than I am. Just let me make a final point. I am not here today to judge you. That judgment will be dictated by your own actions. I am here today to appeal to you for more common sense, to try to save all of your lives. We are rightly concerned that there are still some small pockets of unbelievers out there. It is only your people who have but two short years left until the deadline, and then the judgment will come. I hope you will make the right choice. Thank you for listening, and I hope you have heard everything I've said to you. I appeal to you from the bottom of my heart, not to let this happen."

She put her helmet on and then stepped back and disappeared.

Peter Jensen sat in stunned silence at the revelation. Helen—his Helen—was Charlie's wife. She was an alien who had deceived him into believing she cared for him.

Peter was determined to find out was going on. The only thing he could think of was to try to track down her movements during the time she had asked him for an interview. He called Art World, which was happy to hear from him, and indicated that they would be interested in a story featuring his art. But when he asked about the interview he had had with H. H. Banyon, they told him that they did not have a staffer or a freelancer by that name. Even the name Helen Banyon did not appear on their list of contributors.

Peter was at a loss of what to do, until he remembered a friend from school who was successful in the cyber-security field. He wasn't sure that his friend's email address was still valid, but he sent the email, detailing the circumstances of his encounter with Helen. As he emailed his friend the details, he felt foolish chasing after a woman who had deceived him.

As it turned out, his friend's email address was valid. His friend was surprised to hear from him after such a long time, but was also pleased for the renewed contact. He agreed to help.

The first thing he initiated was a cyber-campaign to locate any men who might have had sex with a beautiful woman who had spent the night and disappeared afterwards. The results were spectacular and beyond their wildest expectations. Thousands of men responded to the request, most saying that they were upset or despondent that they could not find the woman again, no matter how hard they tried. Their stories were so alike, with the exception of the physical description of the women in question, that it became obvious that some kind of conspiracy was going on.

Peter, aided by his friend, documented the facts told to him by hundreds of men willing to withstand the rigors of being hounded by the press at every turn. This took several days, many emails, and several long-distant phone conversations, and in the end, the reams of paper produced from every source threatened to overflow the small apartment. It was amazing the amount of detail these love-stricken men were willing to divulge. A timeline was established, the stories simplified, and a final manuscript printed out. Because he was sure Helen was Donna, Peter decided to call it *The Alien Conspiracy.*

Over the next few weeks, Peter submitted the story to dozens of news sites, magazines, and TV stations.

Without proof, none were interested in the speculation.

YEAR 9

PART 1

The One World Council meeting scheduled for late January was postponed until the beginning of March due to a rough winter season, the first in many years. The meeting was delayed to the beginning of May, at Charlie's request, citing lack of acceptable progress. The meeting was held on May 20th. Everybody was able to rearrange their schedules, and all the leaders of the various regions of the world were present, but for some it was difficult to hold back that they felt they were being jerked around.

Charlie stood at the podium in the center of the room. "Welcome to you all. This is our ninth year together, and the fourth year of the One World Council. I have come to encourage you to continue down your chosen path, which is finally showing signs of correcting the current situation. Promises have been made and accepted, and for the most part, have been kept. The leaders of the world have been meeting regularly to try to produce an enforceable document which is acceptable to everyone, including us. The news is good, up to a certain point, but we still have holdouts in certain trouble spots. This is to be expected since not everyone puts the same values on the rights, or even the existence, of individual human lives. There are still men in the world who refuse to give women the same rights as they give themselves. I wish to express my disgust with these individuals who cannot see anything beyond their own self-interest. The rights of all people, men and women, are the same, and the sooner you realize and accept that fact, the sooner we can leave you to enjoy the peace your planet will have. I am also here to remind you of the deadline, which is fast approaching, and will not be altered."

Charlie gripped either side of the lectern, and glared at the members.

"Obviously, since there has been no consensus, and there is no bill before this council, there will be no voting at this meeting. I could see this coming, and that is the reason I delayed the meeting, to give you more time to come with a resolution. Now all I can do is to encourage you to double down on your efforts to get something down on paper which is acceptable to everyone. Burn the midnight oil if you have to, but get it done."

With a final glower and shake of his head, he faded from sight.

Not a sound escaped the hall, apart from the scraping of chairs as they stood to leave.

Rear Admiral Chaffee "Bull" Browning sat behind his huge desk in his office on the third floor of the Pentagon in Washington, D.C. He looked worried, and for good reason. By a stroke of the worst luck, he'd been chosen as the officer in charge of determining the fate of the excess number of soldiers, airmen, and sailors currently serving in the armed forces.

Next year, what I determine won't matter a rat's ass since the world is going to end up incinerated in a huge fireball.

Bull was a dedicated pessimist who believed that nothing was going to change the nature of humanity's prejudices and hatred for those they considered inferior to themselves. Therefore, in his opinion, the inevitable conclusion for Earth was that it would go out with a big bang.

After a few moment's contemplation, he got back to the task at hand. It seemed that this was his lot in life, shuffling papers that meant little to him, but for the armed forces, determined the fate of a great number of men and women in the four branches. Some of the determinations were for the better, but most of the plans were to the detriment of those unfortunate enough to have been chosen to be discharged.

Toward the middle of the afternoon, Bull decided he wanted some refreshment, and rose slowly from his desk. He wasn't as spry as he had been during what he laughingly called *active* duty, when he had been in charge of a battle group.

With a nuclear aircraft carrier as his flagship, he had cruised the Pacific and Indian Oceans, with the knowledge that whatever was thrown in his direction, he could handle it with grace, guts, and glory. The members of his battle group were the best trained and most motivated group of people that he could make them. This showed up in the ever-increasing number of war games his battle group had participated in and won with ease toward the end of his career at sea.

He sighed, knowing that this accomplishment was the main reason he had been kicked upstairs and reassigned to the Pentagon.

Bull stood and exited his office, surprised to find nobody at the desk in the reception area, until he remembered, with a pang of regret, the departure of his secretary of two years. Sharing the rear admiral's pessimism for the human race, thirty-year-old Major Samantha Worthington—*Izzy* to her friends—had resigned her commission, determined to hike the Appalachian Trail from Springer Mountain in Georgia to Mount Katahdin in Maine. She had explained her decision to him as wanting to accomplish something that she could be proud of before becoming just another crispy critter.

He had tried his best to talk her out of going, but had settled for making her promise to carry the satellite phone he had given her, explaining that there were many places along the trail that were out of cell phone range, and he wanted to keep in touch with her to gauge her progress. That phone had subsequently been found in a rented locker at Amicalola Falls State Park, the start of the approach path to Springer Mountain, which was where the Appalachian Trail officially started.

While the rear admiral had had his share of flings and dalliances in his younger days, he had never married, reserving his love and trust to the Navy, the ships, and the sailors who served under him. Now in his late fifties, he had been surprised to find a new secretary in place of the older one, who had been mustered out due to age.

Izzy had immediately won his heart, not only for her competence at her job, but for her bright and cheery disposition, and also the veiled suggestions she made when no one else was around. It did take a few months of suggestions, innuendo, and outright requests, but finally they ended up in bed together. It was against the long-standing rules of the Navy, of course, but through discretion and subterfuge, their first fling soon turned into a long-standing affair which neither party regretted.

As Bull exited the office and moved into the corridor, he wasn't surprised at the lack of personnel sharing the space. The drawdown of uniformed officers had been going on for several years now, ever since the aliens had removed the reasons for wars, as well as the means to fight those battles. This was the main reason that he was shuffling papers.

Lost in thought, he wandered the many corridors of the Pentagon for several hours, forgetting why he had left his office, but still ended up at the cafeteria. He grabbed a cup of coffee and a cheese Danish, and with his mind still in a whirl, returned to his office.

Damn, he was going to miss that girl.

Sam "Izzy" Worthington stood on the bridge of the aliens' flagship, receiving several reports from her duty stations throughout the fleet. In this particular Navy, she was not a major, but the fleet Flagship commander, second-in-command to Charlie. She had fought her way up to that position from being just a raw recruit, and had been satisfied in her current position, until she had seen the glow on the faces of the female seekers who had completed their missions and had come home pregnant. These women were held in high regard by the entire fleet.

Determined to share in their success and to experience the joys of motherhood, she had lobbied Charlie for many years to be allowed to become a seeker herself. When the call for more women volunteers went out, she had once again presented herself to Charlie, determined not to be put off again.

Reluctant for a long time to allow his second-in-command to expose herself to the inherent dangers of such a deception, Charlie finally acquiesced to her requests, but set it up in a way that she would be in minimal danger during her two-year mission.

She was checking yet another report with approval, when Charlie slipped behind her and laid a hand on her shoulder.

"I've heard from the doctor. He tells me you are having twins. Congratulations are in order, I think."

"Thank you, sir. I feel proud of the result of the mission."

On duty, Sam always followed protocol, and addressed him as *sir*, or *commander.* Off duty, he was a true friend, along with his wife.

"The hell with the mission, I want you to be proud that you are a mother-to-be, and you will soon feel that pride in your children."

"I already do."

"I have told all the other pregnant women that they are relieved of any duty other than to themselves and their children. However, with you, I will leave it up to your own judgment as to when you need to step down from command in order to safeguard your twins."

"Thank you once again, sir. I promise not to endanger myself or the twins." She turned and looked Charlie in the eyes.

Charlie, with a smile on his face and a twinkle in his eyes, turned and headed back to his ready room.

PART 2

In the back streets of Mumbai, India, a stealthy figure stole down a dark alley. Mohammad Abadi, *Mo* to his few friends, was an accomplished beggar and thief, having kept himself alive and reasonably comfortable for the last nine of his fifteen years.

He could not read or write, never having attended school, since his parents had been killed in one of the food riots which had occurred with monotonous regularity in the many impoverished nations of the world before Charlie put an end to them.

Mo knew of the aliens because one of their ships was parked twenty thousand feet above Mumbai. What he didn't know was why they were here, since he didn't own a TV or radio, and didn't know anyone who did.

Something strange was going on. Something he could not comprehend, and that made him suspicious. Mo had just returned to his familiar neighborhood from an excursion toward the center of the city, and what he saw there and on the way back was incomprehensible. He had observed many people going into several stores, picking out what they wanted, and walking out without paying. What was the strangest, though, was that the smiling store owner was standing there watching them leave and making no move to stop them or even call the police.

Keeping a watchful eye for anyone who would steal from him, Mo carried a large bag of groceries, made up of the best, most expensive items he could find, which he had selected and taken from the local market, with the smiling owner in view. Although he was well-known to this owner, who had called the police on Mo many times, the man had allowed him to leave with his bag, even patted him on his head as he left the store. It felt strange walking away slowly instead of sprinting.

Mo was more than halfway down the alley, headed toward the basement of an abandoned building he called home, when he halted, his acute senses telling him that he was not alone any more. He glanced backward, toward the entrance by which he had come into the alley, but there was nothing. He turned forward again to continue his journey, but before he could take another step, he was confronted by a huge figure who appeared out of nowhere. The man was dressed in all black and wore a black full-face helmet with a tinted visor.

Mo stumbled back several steps.

"Mo, just relax, I'm not here to hurt you." The voice rumbled from behind the visor.

Mo felt his legs become rubbery. "Get away from me! I didn't steal this. It was given to me."

"I know, because I was there." The huge man raised his visor to reveal a smooth black face with a benevolent smile.

"I didn't see you there."

"No, you didn't, because I was invisible. No one saw me."

"Yeah, right, you were invisible. I'm not a fool. No one can do that."

The man blinked out, and returned five seconds later.

"Wha-what do you want with me?"

"I want to help you. I know you didn't learn to read or write, so I want to help you to understand what is going on, and explain to you why you don't have to live in that basement by yourself any longer. I am here to educate you on how to live."

Mo stood with glazed-over eyes. Never in his short life had anyone offered to help him.

"Tell you what," the man rumbled. "Why don't we go to your home, and I will explain everything to you." He turned and strode down the center of the alley, toward Mo's basement.

Mo followed while keeping a comfortable distance between them.

PART 3

"I never thought I would see this castle, my namesake, built all those years ago, but here we are."

The young couple stood hand-in-hand on the Mariannebruck Bridge, overlooking the edifice that was Neuschwanstein Castle in Southern Bavaria, Germany.

"What do you mean, Ludwig?"

His beautiful bride of two weeks was not a student of history and was not familiar with the splendor of what they were viewing on their honeymoon.

"This glorious Romanesque revival castle was built by Mad King Ludwig, starting in 1869, and was finally finished in 1886. But unfortunately, the king was drowned in that lake over there only seven weeks before it was completed."

Ludwig was a history major at university.

"Well, it is gorgeous, of course, but you said we were going to Oktoberfest, like the one we went to in Helen, Georgia."

One thing he did like about his new bride was her love of beer.

"Julie, we will go to Oktoberfest, but it's in Munich and doesn't start for another week. I thought we would look around the Alps beforehand, and then go there. We already have the reservations."

He put his arm around her shoulders and squeezed her, and her petite body relaxed as he rolled her around to face him, the bent down to deliver a romantic kiss. She snaked her arms around his waist and pulled him tight against her body, experiencing once again the thrill of the nights they had spent together on this honeymoon.

"Are you serious?" she said. "Do you really want to see the inside of the castle, where a long-dead, mentally incompetent king spent his last days. Or would you rather retire to our room with a live woman who wants to play?"

"Tell you what. I'll make a deal with you. If we do the inside tour right now, we can spend all day tomorrow inside the hotel room. We can even order room service. This castle is the one I have been waiting to see all my life, and this will be my one chance, given the aliens' ultimatum. What do you think?"

Her expression went from annoyance to shy compliance.

"OK, deal," she whispered.

The tour was comprehensive for the student of history, but Julie thought the furnishings and decorations were excessive, expensive, ugly, and gauche. As soon as the tour guide found out that the man's name was Ludwig, he showed them spaces the normal tourist wasn't aware of, and the couple ended up spending much more time in the castle than they had planned.

"You know," the guide said, "my name was Ludwig, too, back in the day. Back when I was playing Mad King Ludwig."

"Oh, I didn't realize they held reenactments here. And just when was that?"

With a huge grin, the guide said, "Oh, back in the 1870s and '80s. And I wasn't playing a role, I actually was Mad King Ludwig."

"Impossible!"

"It is not only possible, but true. I am one of the aliens, and I have been here on Earth for over two hundred years, playing many personages over those years, one of which was Mad King Ludwig. I liked that role. But I must admit, some of the people I portrayed were not as nice or as famous. But you would be surprised to learn just how many famous people were actually us in disguise."

"You have got to be kidding me, right?"

"No, I am definitely not. And you would realize it if you just stop and think about it. Why would Mozart, who was Austrian, and Ludwig, who was German, have such a close and long-lasting friendship? How did they meet, and what kept them coming back together, time after time, in the most obscure places?"

"You tell me. I don't know."

"OK, I'll tell you how it was back then. Both Mozart and I, as Mad King Ludwig, were aliens. And not only that, on the ship during the journey here from our home world, we were bunkmates and formed our friendship on that ship. He is still here as well. Although, I will admit that over the last few years, I have lost track of him. However, I can guarantee the both of us will be leaving with the ships when they go away at the end of next year."

"So, if you were there in 1886, when Ludwig died, did you drown, or were you murdered, as some historians claim?"

"Neither, actually. I did go into the lake, and I did go under the water, but I was transported to my ship, leaving the people to speculate about the manner of my death, since no body was ever found. I wish there had been another way for me to go, but that was what was decided higher up in the chain of command."

Ludwig turned toward Julie with a puzzled look and saw the shock on her face. The turn caused him to lose sight of their guide for a few seconds, and when he turned back, the man was gone, leaving them deep in the dungeon level of the castle. No amount of shouting or searching revealed a sign of the guide, so they traveled back up to the castle proper.

They were surprised to find that, apart from the two security guards at the main gate, they were the only people in the castle. The two guards ushered them out and slammed the gates behind them.

Leaving the castle way past closing time, the couple was dismayed to find that the last shuttle down the mountain had left ten minutes earlier. But since it was a balmy evening, their stroll down the mountain road in the darkness wasn't daunting. Halfway down they encountered a premium restaurant and bar, and had their evening meal there.

"So, do you believe what he was saying about him being King Ludwig?" Julie said.

"I don't know. He was much more knowledgeable than you would expect the normal tour guide to be, but the story still seems unbelievable. Mind you, I didn't believe in aliens from outer space until the facts were shoved in my face."

"But if he were telling the truth, how many of the famous and talented people in our past were actually aliens playing their roles and manipulating humanity toward certain directions?"

"You, my girl, are a lot smarter than people give you credit for. I don't know, and I doubt if we ever will, unless the aliens themselves are willing to enlighten us, which is doubtful." Ludwig just sat and stared at his food.

Julie grinned. "Don't forget your promise, lover boy. Now finish up, and let's get going."

It was after eleven when they finally arrived at their hotel. As they climbed the four flights of stairs to their room, because the elevator had broken down earlier due to the excessive weight of a group of German tuba players, they realized that the day's excursions, along with an excess of German beer, had taken a toll on their reserves, and they were both huffing and puffing by the time they reached their door.

They poured into their room, and Ludwig walked over to the overstuffed couch, grabbing the TV remote on his way. After he thumbed the TV on, his attention was grabbed by Julie, who, after locking the door, dropped her jacket on the floor, ripped her T-shirt off over her head, unfastened her lace bra, and threw it at him.

"For the next twenty-four hours, buster, your ass is mine," she growled.

She threw her jeans and panties onto the floor on her way over to the couch, and by the time she arrived, he was more than ready for her.

The next day was a blur. Ludwig had awoken that morning all ready and raring to go. He knew their next destination was Oktoberfest in Munich. He had been alone in the bed, but reasoned that she was in the bathroom. After fifteen minutes relaxing in bed, he grew worried and padded over to the bathroom. The door was slightly ajar, but he knocked anyway.

No answer.

He went inside, and to his surprise it was empty. With growing apprehension, he noted that one of their suitcases was missing, so he crossed the room and opened the closet, only to find that all her clothes were gone. There was no note anywhere, and when he called the front desk, they were not aware that she had departed.

Ludwig called the police, and once they took down all the pertinent information, then started a countrywide search for the missing young woman, who they suspected had been kidnapped.

A week later, still no sign of her. Even an Internet search failed.

Heartbroken Ludwig decided to skip Munich and fly home.

"So, the doctor has confirmed that you are pregnant?" Charlie said to Julie, as they watched the video feed from the hotel room where Ludwig was frantically searching for his bride.

"Yes." She beamed. "Almost a month now."

They watched silently as Ludwig pulled out his cell phone and dialed her number. Her phone started ringing from the bedside table where she had left it when she had been transported back to the ship. He walked into the bedroom, saw her phone sitting there ringing, and burst into tears.

"I don't want to watch any more. I can't take it."

Julie was on the verge of tears herself, despite knowing all along that this was how it was going to end.

Charlie put a protective arm around her shoulder and turned her away from the screen.

For the past month, Ludwig had been searching for clues as to where she had gone. What he'd found had no explanation. The house where she said she had grown up didn't exist. Her schools had no records for her. The places she said she had worked didn't know about her. And worst of all, the government said she didn't exist. No social security number. No passport was ever issued in her name, and the airline they flew to Europe on had only his ticket listed in their database. When he called the German police to check on their progress, he was told that no such case existed in their files.

YEAR 10

PART 1

Sunshine and unusually high temperatures greeted the January day that Charlie had announced for the final meeting of the One World Council. On this day, everything shut down, except emergencies. It was an unofficial holiday on which everyone would find out their ultimate fate.

When Charlie finally arrived, he did so in a way no one expected. Instead of just appearing in the expected place, he flew a small scout ship which landed vertically in the plaza in front of the One World Headquarters.

Charlie was the only person aboard the autonomous ship, capable of planning and managing the height, speed, and route without any intervention. Charlie merely told it where he wanted to go, and from that point he was but a passenger. He used the flight time to put the finishing touches on his speech.

Charlie emerged, surprisingly, without his helmet, allowing his long black hair to blow in the breeze, and his ship left silently. He drifted toward the entrance, stopping occasionally to acknowledge a diplomat who was close. When he finally reached the doors, he turned to smile and wave at the crowd, who clapped and cheered at his presence.

Charlie entered and passed between the leaders. He hesitated as he proceeded down the aisle toward the podium, as if he didn't really want to get there. Once he finally swung onto the dais to face the representatives, he sighed.

"Good morning. As you all know, this is the final year of the allotted time I have been allowed to finalize the solution of the problem facing the Continuum of Planets. While I am sure you will agree that Earth has made a remarkable turnaround from the situation it was in just nine years ago, I fear we have fallen short of the final mark. It was pointed out to me just a short while ago, by my superiors, that there are still small pockets of resistance to the edicts of not only the One World Council, but to the ultimatum the whole world faces at the end of the year."

Charlie surveyed the faces around him. After nine years, he recognized all of them, and had even begun to know how they felt, as well as how they would vote. The expressions he saw ranged from abject embarrassment to anxiousness.

"I am speaking not only to the members of this One World Council, the leaders of the various regions of the world, but also to the entire population of the world, the majority of whom I am sure are listening with rapt attention. Our sophisticated computer systems aboard our ships have noticed several disturbing trends in small pockets, and even with individuals. There appears to be areas where silences speak as loud as words, and indifference is as powerful as outright prejudices. The refusal to participate, or to do business with a person or a class of individuals, is still a symptom of prejudice, no matter how hard you try to disguise it."

Charlie again paused. He hoped someone would interrupt him with a question so he could avoid feeling that he was dictating to the world. But only silence reigned.

"So, beginning tomorrow, our communications officers will be contacting all law enforcement people, all politicians and community leaders, to pinpoint the many small holdouts of non-conformity scattered across the globe, with the hope that if these people are confronted one-on-one they will seriously think about what their prejudices are doing to the planet at large. If for some reason that doesn't work, I am afraid I am out of ideas, and the planet will just have to suffer."

Charlie's smile, ever-present for so long, was now gone, replaced by an ominous mask of concern.

"That is all I have for you today. Good luck with your task, and goodbye."

Charlie blinked out.

PART 2

Ramos Parker was a six-six, muscular black man of two hundred ninety pounds. Why his father had named him Ramos was anyone's guess, and no one was likely to find out since his father was incarcerated on the aliens' prison ship for shooting Ramos's mother seventeen times during a drunken domestic disturbance.

Ramos was an NFL quarterback who entered the league at a late age due to earning a Ph.D. in Internal Medicine, a piece of paper now worthless due to the introduction of the aliens' medical advances.

Those advances had allowed football, and other competitive sports, to elevate from what had been extremely dangerous professions to safe ones. Even players who suffered broken bones or traumatic head injuries were able to play by the following week.

Ramos was admired on the field not only for his brute strength and lightning speed, but for his sharp mind, which allowed him to anticipate the opposition's plays before the ball was snapped. He was also a master at creating scoring opportunities on broken plays.

Off the field, everyone wanted to be around him. He was proof that an individual could come from a dysfunctional upbringing and still emerge as a role model for his peers and the youth. His modest actions and unbiased demeanor made him a friend to all. Even his opponents admired him.

The game itself had evolved since the arrival of the aliens. Penalty flags were eliminated since the players were more skilled instead of relying totally on aggressiveness. Apart from the addition of six new teams, and a longer playing season, the game remained the same. The biggest change was the addition of overseas teams.

Ramos Parker stood at the podium before an assembly of the greatest football players of all time. He surveyed the crowd with awe.

"Ladies and gentlemen, it is with great humility and pride that I stand before you tonight. On such a momentous and memorable occasion, I find myself thinking back over the past year and wondering where we all would be today had it not been for the arrival of the aliens, who have transformed the whole world."

He scanned the multitude below him.

"Obviously, I don't know your thoughts on the matter, but I believe that the world would be dead by now had it not been for their intervention."

He paused again.

"It has been an amazing season for us all, not only for the winners, but for all the competitors who put up the good fight."

Football wasn't the only sport that had been transformed. Baseball, basketball, hockey, and motor sports were also affected by the hordes of fans that flocked to the stadiums every weekend, taking advantage of the free admission.

Formula One Racing continued unabated, providing its adherents with the spectacle it had always been, as individual drivers vied for the coveted World Champion Driver's Title, and teams for the Constructor of the Year Title. The top teams were still Mercedes, Ferrari, and Red Bull, but with even younger drivers.

The cars, which now had no wheels, no longer raced on a track, but flew around a course at a maximum of fifty feet, passing through holographically projected gates, in highly developed versions of Hover cars. The racecar drivers were protected by limited time versions of the aliens' shields, and were therefore impervious to harm. But the cars could be, and often were, destroyed. Anyone abusing this technology was imprisoned after the event and was banned from racing forever.

The IndyCar and NASCAR programs were similar except for the manufacturers and style of the vehicles. All cars were still covered with many sponsor advertisements. Even though there was no money to change hands, all the advertisers wanted to keep their names and slogans in the forefront of the public's mind.

An interesting aspect that came about was the introduction of Retro Racing, and all three disciplines participated. These were 2020-era cars, the only modification being the aliens' forcefield shield protecting each driver, so fans and drivers who longed for the *good old days* could indulge to their heart's content.

Steven Garrison sighed heavily, for he was at last a happy man. While working his twelve-year career at the Post Office, he was hated every minute of his boring life and dreamed of the day he would finally be able to indulge in his fantasy occupation. Today, his vision of his future came to fruition.

All of his life, he'd wanted to be a brewer. He had learned all the facts and nuances of the art of brewing, and wanted to start his own brewery. But he had always run into the same problem over and over again.

He had no money.

Now, with the aliens' declaration that there would be no money, he was free to embark upon his dream.

Steven was not looking to challenge the major breweries. His was to be a small operation, a nano-brewery, which would be offering only four styles of craft beer created to his own specifications. He envisioned having a light amber beer, an English style IPA, a Belgian triple, and a dark stout. He only wanted to brew about fifteen gallons of each so he could change and refine the recipes at any time. He enjoyed experimenting.

Steven was unmarried with no children, and did not have a steady girlfriend since his demeanor had been pessimistic due to his hatred of the life he was living. His parents, both professors at the University of New Delhi, had been overseas when they had been caught up in the food riots which plagued the lower castes in India, and they were both killed by a crazed mob of starving people who saw them as rich foreigners who were withholding food from the general population. So, he was alone in the world.

His mood and outlook on life had improved immensely because the aliens' arrival had given him the opportunity to live out his dreams. He had already managed to acquire some land near the Blue Ridge Mountains in North Carolina, and it even came with a building in which to live, and was large enough to accommodate his small brewery.

His first job was to construct a building for storage of the beer ingredients, with an attached bar/pub, lounge and entertainment area. He envisioned live music played by local bands or individuals, performing on weekends for the imbibers of his craft beers.

He even imagined that his land was sufficient to accommodate a distillery and a winery, with lots of land left over for the vines to grow. Now, all he had to do was to find the necessary people who had the combination of knowledge and inspiration to help him achieve his goals.

Life was finally good, and it was about to get even better.

PART 3

Toward the middle of that final year, Charlie announced that a worldwide broadcast would occur the following week, and urged the world's population to tune in.

Although speculation ran rampant, it was agreed that this was when the people would learn the fate of Earth.

At the appointed time, Charlie's visage appeared on every TV set and computer in the world.

"Greetings, people of Earth." Charlie said. "I come before you today to announce that shortly we will be departing your world and returning to ours to wait for the next crisis to appear. While no date and time has yet been set, this event will occur sometime before the end of the current year. You will know that it has come to pass by the absence of our ships in your skies. While, on occasion, our time here has been contentious, overall, we are pleased with the progress the human race has made toward becoming an acceptable candidate for inclusion into the Continuum of Planets.

"Now, of course, we come to the ultimatum. Those who for the past ten years have been wondering if Earth could transform itself into a world which would be acceptable enough to us in order to avoid destruction, will finally have an answer."

His face broke into a smile, one which became infectious. His eyes crinkled at the corners, and the world held its collective breath.

"After a great deal of discussion and deliberation, we have decided that Earth has made enough progress to be spared the ultimate sacrifice of total destruction. We find that if the planet's population can continue on the course we have implemented, we believe that ultimately this will be one of the best planets in the continuum, and we fervently hope that mankind has finally seen that to cooperate and compromise is much better than to conflict and compete with one another."

A collective sigh of relief could be heard across the world, followed by cheering and partying.

"Next month, free and impartial elections will be held, to choose from each region of Earth—formally known as countries—a person who will represent that region as a member of the One World Council. Those chosen people will then vote to elect the supreme leader of the world, or whichever title that person wants. Each member of the Council will have an advisory panel to help with the organization of their particular region, subject to the approval of the supreme leader. When it's your turn to vote, choose wisely. Everyone over the age of eighteen will be eligible to vote, no exceptions, and will be expected to do so. The popular vote will prevail, no matter which or how many organizations attempt to spin it differently."

All TVs returned to their regular programming.

EPILOGUE

PART 1

In early September, the elections were held all around the world. Not surprisingly, most of the previous leaders, representing regions of Earth which were formally countries, were reelected to the One World Council.

When the Council met again in late September, the first item on the agenda was the election of the supreme leader. While Charlie was not present, most suspected he was keeping a surreptitious eye on the proceedings.

As expected, when the votes were finally counted, every leader had cast a vote for himself or herself, and a quandary emerged. No one knew how to break the stalemate, and it seemed that the aliens' representative, Charlie, would have to intervene once more in the proceedings.

There was much discussion about what to do, before the Canadian prime minister stood and waved for silence.

"I wish to change my vote. Since Canada and the United States of America share the majority of the continent of North America, and since the two countries have always had a close and sympathetic relationship, I now wish to cast my vote in favor of the president of the United States, Sylvia Han-Chin. This will give her a fifty-percent majority over all other candidates."

The assembly broke into an uproar. Questions and accusations rained down like hellfire, and everyone was shouting at the top of their voices. After fifteen minutes of pandemonium, Sylvia stood and marched to the podium, where she picked up the gavel and brought it down three times, the strident sound reverberating throughout the chamber. Everyone became silent, and turned their gazes toward her.

"Thank you. I accept the vote and the position."

Mouths hung agape, and many heads shook in amazement, but there was no argument. Along with many others, even Boris wore a big grin. He looked forward to their future confrontations.

In his command center aboard his ship, Charlie nodded. He had always liked and admired Sylvia for her fortitude and resilience, and thought the nomination was a smart and prudent choice. He looked forward to their last meeting.

Sylvia stood at the podium, gavel in hand, and watched as all the members slowly seated themselves.

"Thank you one and all for the opportunity to serve you. I promise to treat each human with the same respect and courtesy, the same concern and dignity, that everyone deserves. I will attempt to hold myself and this office to a higher standard than all others, and if I fail to do so, there will be another election in five years, where another can take over from me. I now declare this election over."

Thunderous applause broke out, led by Boris.

PART 2

The day after the election, Sylvia was sitting in the Oval Office, contemplating how she was going to carry the extra workload she had brought upon herself, when her thoughts were interrupted by a rap on the door. Knowing that particular cadence, she smiled as she invited him in.

Ben Williamson strode in with his usual gusto. “Sylvia, we have to talk.”

“Yes, Ben, I know what you are going to say. Why did I volunteer for this, right?”

“Something along those lines, yes.”

“I’ve been thinking it over, and I’ve come to a conclusion.”

“Which is?”

“I’m going to ask the American people to allow the vice president to take over my duties here in the White House, and for you to take my chair at the One World Council since Charlie so thoughtfully provided me with a throne to sit upon.”

During election day, an oversized chair that Charlie considered a suitably grand throne, had been transported to a place of prominence inside the Council chambers. It was gaudy to Sylvia, but she had accepted the gift with aplomb.

"I think that's a good plan," Ben said. "I find it acceptable, and I think the vice president would, too, if it is endorsed by the American people."

Sylvia vanished before his eyes.

He looked around, but saw nothing. *Charlie.*

One moment, Sylvia was talking to Ben, and the next she was facing Charlie, who sat in an impressive captain's chair similar to the throne she had received at the Council Chambers. He wore a broad smile, and was holding out his hands in greeting.

"Sylvia. So nice of you to drop by."

She smiled back. "I don't think I had much of a choice. But I am glad to see you, since I doubted you would leave without a final meeting."

"Ah, Sylvia, perceptive as usual, I see. I wanted this meeting with you to lay out some facts and a timetable for our imminent departure. I also wanted a chance to talk to you face to face without others present."

"May I sit?"

"But of course. Excuse me for being so forgetful."

Charlie rose and took her arm to guide her to a small chaise lounge, and sat beside her.

"Please be comfortable, Sylvia. I mean you no harm. In fact, I must say that I was extremely pleased when they chose you as their supreme leader. I cannot think of anyone else who is more suited to the position than you are, even though we are aware of the actions you and Amos were involved in early in your career concerning a former holder of your position."

It took all her willpower for Sylvia not to blush at his praise. Only moments before, she had been doubting her ability to handle all the extra duties on her plate.

"We will be leaving soon," Charlie said. "But we will be leaving behind all the infrastructure, technology, and innovations we have given you. We hope you will use them well. I have one warning, and several revelations, though."

Uh-oh. Here it comes.

"We will be returning a hundred years from now to replace the power cells, which will be at the end of their cycle by then. At that time, we will also be checking up on how you are doing as far as the progress, or lack thereof, you have made in the intervening years. If we come back and find that the majority of the human race has reverted to the situation we found ten years ago, we will have no choice but to carry out our original solution to the problem, and exterminate the planet. If we find that it is a minority, we will work to correct the problem with the people who are alive at that time, which fortunately, will include you."

"What exactly is that supposed to mean?" Sylvia replied. "Despite all the advanced medicine and procedures you have given us, I still cannot believe that I will be alive in a hundred years."

"Without the technology of our longevity, our shields, our invisibility, or our transporters, which we are not leaving behind, all human beings will have a slightly longer lifespan than they enjoy today. Some may even get an extra twenty-five, but not an extra hundred years. But you are different from them. You see, you are one of us, conceived here on Earth by a human man and an alien mother, and implanted with the chip at birth. You were the first viable baby from this combination."

"What are you trying to tell me?"

"That you will be here when we return in a hundred years, but the people alive today will not."

"You have no concept of what human doctors are capable of once they get their teeth into a problem." *Especially now that they're actually working on the root of illnesses, and not worried about getting paid off medications.* "You are placing the success of this planet in my lap, whether or not I want it?"

"I'm afraid so. In the past ten years, I have not found anyone more capable than you. However, there does exist the possibility that you will fail. Nevertheless, I wish you and your people the best of luck in managing your baser instincts and becoming a model planet, one which will be welcomed into the Continuum of Planets with open arms. Now that I have scared the living daylights out of you, I want to leave you with something that is for your ears only, and for those who subsequently take over your position. Do I have your solemn oath that what I am about to tell you will never be repeated to any person except your successor?"

Sylvia nodded. "On a stack of Bibles, I so swear."

Charlie grinned. "In that case, what I have to tell you may come as a surprise. Or it may not, given your level of perception. Our main mission here on Earth was to ensure the viability of your planet. But we also had a secondary mission, one which I am pleased to tell you, has succeeded beyond our wildest dreams. Due to an industrial accident on my planet over two hundred years ago, all males of my species are impotent." Charlie gazed deep into her eyes as he revealed the deceptions that had occurred over the past ten years. "During our time here, many of the females on our ships have made excursions onto your planet for the express purpose of getting pregnant so our race would not die out. As I indicated before, we have had impressive success with this program, with over fifteen thousand babies and fetuses, all of them viable. While there have been rumors of our program, and even one enterprising man who put it all together, our secret has only been revealed to you."

Sylvia jumped to her feet and hovered over Charlie.

He leaned backward.

"I vehemently protest your actions in the kidnapping of all these Earth babies."

Charlie stood and gently seated her again, and then sat beside her.

"I know this has come as a shock to you, but we simply had no choice. Of all the planets in the Continuum, yours is the only one we have found to be compatible with ours. And even then, it is only half-compatible. If you remember all those men who died on my ships. They were killed by the genetic defect of combining with the DNA of your females. While some of your males may feel a sense of loss over the female who has disappeared, all the babies are with their mother and will never want for anything. Even your courts have given precedent to the mothers over custody of children. This was the bad part of my revelation to you. But there is a good part, too. Knowing that my people and my ships are invulnerable, and that for the last million Earth years we have had no enemies, it would probably not surprise you that we have no offensive weapons. We haven't had them for a million years. Besides, our moral code would not allow us to use them even if we had them. Therefore, you can see that we are not capable of blowing up another ship, let alone a planet. This has been a bluff on our part, but we have found that the threat of destruction works just as well as the ability to carry out that threat, as long as the population believes it. This is why I have to insist that you do not mention this information to anyone except your immediate successor. Not even to Ben or Boris. Do I have your word on that?"

Sylvia stood open-mouthed, while she processed the information.

"Yes, of course you have my word," she finally said.

Charlie smiled. "Then my lady, I bid you a fond farewell, and I'll see you in one hundred years."

She found herself back in the Oval Office, facing Ben Williamson, now on his third whiskey.

"Charlie?" he said.

"Charlie!"

PART 3

December 25th, a holiday still celebrated even though religion ceased to exist, brought a welcome change to the world, one that everyone noticed the moment they awoke.

The alien ships were gone. Those huge discs which had dominated the skies above the cities around the world for the past ten years were now gone. Christmas had a new miracle to celebrate.

Warren DuPont, alone in his bedroom in Denver, knew something was different the moment he awoke that Christmas morning. His bedroom windows, facing east, were bright with the morning sun, which he not seen for past ten years.

He grabbed his robe and rushed outside to join the others looking skyward. The ship was gone. It had disappeared during the night without a sound.

Warren wasn't the only one who felt a chill of apprehension about what was going to happen now that the aliens were no longer watching over the planet.

Amos Richardson first heard the news on TV as he drank his morning coffee. Being far from a major city, he noticed no difference in his surroundings, and hoped it stayed that way.

As soon as he heard the news, Craig Simmons rushed from the restaurant and looked up. Sure enough, the dark ship which had dominated the Miami skies twenty miles south had gone as if it had never been there. Relief mixed with worry over his missing fiancé dominated his mind.

The aliens could no longer aid him for his search for her, but he vowed to find her someday.

It was with a pang of regret that Paul Johnson heard the jubilant news of the aliens' departure that Christmas morning, knowing one of those ships was carrying away the young lady he had rescued. He walked outside and gazed up at the empty sky, wondering how far she had already been carried away from him.

A new career in designing computer games and programming subroutines for the city now occupied the majority of Richard

Adams's life, although he did find time to converse with his new friends in the computer world. Because of his new occupation, he hardly noticed the departure of the alien ships, but was grateful for their intervention. He was still working with numbers, after all.

A year later, military authorities finally contacted Jerry Sanders with the report they had received from the aliens about the accidental shooting of children in Afghanistan. It had been decided that since it happened so long ago, and since he had led an exemplary since then, that he be allowed to continue helping orphans find loving parents. He was thankful for the aliens' handling of the situation, and for the common sense of the authorities.

Jason Stein sat motionless for a long time, realizing that he had lost a good friend in Joe, his alien minder. Jason's sole reminder from their time together was the LTLE-1 laser gun, now encased in a block of resin displayed on the mantelpiece above his fireplace. The two had enjoyed many meetings together, attempting to work out the world's problems. He knew those meetings were being reported back to Charlie, but since they were all working toward the same goal, no action was ever taken against him.

He was going miss those sessions with Joe, not only for his sensibilities, but for his wry sense of humor, something unexpected from an alien.

Fishing had been good for Tommy Hernandez, who had filled his government quota in just a few hours. The king mackerel in his holds was going to make a large quantity of smoked kingfish dip, one of Tommy's favorites.

As the sun rose above the horizon, he turned his boat toward Miami and looked for his waypoint mark, but the huge black alien ship he had relied on as a marker for the past ten years was gone. He scanned the horizon, but there was no sign of it. He turned on his GPS and radio, and received not only directions to get to Miami, but the news that explained the absence of his mark.

Tommy felt a pang of loss. The aliens had helped everyone on Earth, and had saved the world. He could not be more grateful to them than he felt at that moment if he lived to be a hundred years old.

In Georgetown, Josh Jackson and Harry Miller lingered over their morning cup of coffee, watching through the floor, to ceiling picture windows, at the empty sky which just the day before had held the giant black alien spaceship.

"Well it seems that the aliens were satisfied at our attempts to rid the world of the prejudice that has been a part of our history for so long." Josh said.

"If only we played some small part in making it happen." Harry helped himself to another one of his cook's hot buttered scones, along with a dab of raspberry jam.

Peter self-published *The Alien Conspiracy* since no publisher would touch it with a ten-foot pole. He was sitting in the corner of the room, with all one thousand copies of it. It seemed no one wanted to read about what may have been the greatest kidnapping in human history. Since he did not have all the verifiable facts, legitimate news reporting services shied away from any involvement in the conjecture.

He was saddened, because despite all the detailed accounts he had collected, which to him seemed conclusive not only for the human race, but to him personally for the woman he had lost.

Driving to work that Christmas morning, Captain Alan Jamison could not help but notice the absence of the black ship above Miami. Since the only contact he had been granted by the aliens involved their extensive computer systems, his only feeling of loss was for the ease with which he had been able to obtain information. Even as he felt gladdened at the threat being gone, he vowed to do all he could to upgrade the police systems for future generations.

Unmarried with no living relatives, Alan had been saving as much as he could, but he had no clue why. Of course, it didn't matter because there was no money any more. He was due to retire soon, but had no idea what he wanted to do with his time.

Chaffee "Bull" Browning had greeted that Christmas morning in an unusual fashion. Upon rising, he poured a large glass of bourbon, buoying a single ice cube within its space, and walked outside into the light snowfall, in his pajamas and bedroom slippers. He raised the glass skyward, saluting the empty space the alien ship had occupied.

Actually, he was saying goodbye to Izzy, for he was now convinced that she had left him behind. After the satellite phone had been located, he had spent months at the many access points to the Appalachian Trail, questioning hikers and trail angels, as well as motel owners and forest service personnel as to her whereabouts. Nobody had seen her, and when he checked her service record, he hit another blank wall. There was no record of her anywhere. Having seen how beautiful Charlie's wife, Donna, was, he finally had to admit that Izzy was probably an alien.

Bull carried the half-finished drink inside and sat before a roaring fire with a deep frown and a mind filled with sorrow, contemplating what might have been.

Although he had been living at the orphanage for a while, Mo still had only a vague understanding of what had happened to the world during his lifetime. All he knew was that he was now in a better place. He was better fed with regular nutritional meals, gaining weight at an alarming rate, and going to a school that was teaching him things he had not even fathomed. But his education did not have an explanation of who the aliens were, only that they were good and were responsible for his good fortune.

What bummed him out, though, was that people told him they were gone.

This Christmas morning should have been their first one together, but Ludwig was still experiencing so much distress that the disappearance of the alien ship above his head barely registered in his grief-stricken mind. It took a call from his parents to finally snap him out of his funk and to begin thinking straight.

He began to suspect that only the aliens' technology had the ability to wipe a person's record off the face of the Earth like this. He also suspected that he would never see his bride again, because she was probably speeding away from him at the speed of light.

Ramos Parker was saddened to see the aliens' ships disappear from over the Chicago skies because they were the ones whose edicts had allowed him, and so many others like him, to flourish in whatever field they chose. With his upbringing and his father's disdain and drunken behavior toward not only his mother, but the people in general, Ramos would never have had the chance to shine in academics or athletics.

He was grateful for their help, and vowed on his mother's grave to uphold and to fight against all opposition to the advantages the aliens had given the world.

Finally, every person's life was worth living.

When the ships left, Steven Garrison had already found people who would help him achieve his life's dream. Upward of two hundred qualified individuals worked not *for*, but *with* him to achieve his dream of bringing to the world the finest beers, wines, and spirits it had ever tasted. Since each person's tastes varied, there were going to many more variations of each product than originally imagined.

His plot of land already sported the basic buildings needed to form the core of his imagined empire, and the rest were on the way. The burgeoning vineyard, while still years away from producing crops, had been planted and was under supervision. The stainless-steel tanks for his distillery had been ordered and were on their way, and he looked forward to seeing them installed.

With the help of some good people, who Steven had become friends with, he had been able to collect a set of recipes for every style of beer, wine, and spirits produced in the world, and most of his time was taken up with categorizing, classifying, and modifying them. Because of this, he hardly even noticed the aliens' departure.

Sylvia Han-Chin stood gazing out the window of the Oval Office, into the empty sky. Her eyes glazed over with barely suppressed tears.

Supreme leader of the world…we will have to change that. Sounds so…pompous and dictatorial.

But she couldn't come up with anything better.

How the hell am I going to pull this situation off. I'm only one person, even if I am half-alien.

For Sylvia, both the appointment and the responsibility seemed a hollow victory, for she knew what was going to happen, and it was coming one hundred years down the line.

CayellePublishing.com

COMING SOON

CayellePublishing.com

amazon.com

CayéllePublishing.com

CPSIA information can be obtained
at www.ICGtesting.com
Printed in the USA
LVHW031046290321
682805LV00001B/92

9 781952 404351